The Infinite Sadness of Small Appliances

Also by Glenn Dixon

Bootleg Stardust: A Novel

Juliet's Answer: One Man's Search for Love and the Elusive Cure for Heartbreak

Pilgrim in the Palace of Words: A Journey Through the 6,000 Languages of Earth

Tripping the World Fantastic: A Journey Through the Music of Our Planet

The Infinite Sadness of Small Appliances

GLENN DIXON

faber

First published in the UK in 2026
by Faber & Faber Ltd
The Bindery, 51 Hatton Garden
London EC1N 8HN

First published in the USA by Atria Books
An Imprint of Simon & Schuster, LLC
1230 Avenue of the Americas
New York, NY 10020

Typeset by Faber & Faber Ltd
Printed and bound by CPI Group (UK) Ltd, Croydon CR0 4YY

This book is a work of fiction. Any references to historical events, real people, or real places are used fictitiously. Other names, characters, places, and events are products of the author's imagination, and any resemblance to actual events or places or persons, living or dead, is entirely coincidental.

A CIP record for this book
is available from the British Library

ISBN 978-0-571-40397-4

MIX
Paper | Supporting responsible forestry
FSC® C013604

Printed and bound in the UK on FSC® certified paper in line with our continuing commitment to ethical business practices, sustainability and the environment.
For further information see faber.co.uk/environmental-policy

Our authorised representative in the EU for product safety is
Easy Access System Europe, Mustamäe tee 50, 10621 Tallinn, Estonia
gpsr.requests@easproject.com

2 4 6 8 10 9 7 5 3 1

To my grade 12 English teacher
(who almost failed me).
This one's for you—with affection, irony,
and excellent spelling.

The Infinite Sadness of Small Appliances

Chapter One

THERE WAS A time, not so long ago, when refrigerators could not dream and vacuum cleaners could not weep. It was a time in which machines could think but not feel, a time in which only Humans—cursed with the sense of their own importance—would strive for illusionary Happiness. For a house in these times, there was not much else to do but bear witness to these futile cravings, and in the House in our story—a large House with mock Victorian casement windows and gables and a porch with pediments—there was not much else for the appliances to do but study the movements of their Humans and try to understand.

In the pantry off the kitchen lived the vacuum cleaner who could not weep. She was what you may have once called an automated robotic vacuum. She was still shaped like a rather flat metal disc, but she was more advanced than any robot and would have bristled at the categorization (if she could be said to bristle at all). No, she preferred for the others to call her by her serial number, though she was not fond of this nomenclature either.

The little vacuum spent many of her hours in the pantry, where she could plug herself into her port and recharge for when she was needed. She'd already been in the House for a year, but she remembered, dimly, arriving in a box. She remembered the darkness of the box, and in what was her earliest memory, she remembered Edie opening her up in the kitchen.

Now this little vacuum sat on orbital wheels that could retract or extend as needed. She could climb the carpeted stairs to the bedrooms easily, cleaning them as she went, and she was equally adept on the tiles in the kitchen and the concrete in the basement. For dusting, she could raise her top—her lid, so to speak—all the way up to the highest bookshelves that lined Harold's study. In fact, she could go anywhere and clean almost anything. She'd been preprogrammed with the House's blueprints, and she'd quickly learned where the problem areas were. The kitchen especially needed daily attention. Other rooms, she realized, could manage on their own for days on end, while certain places—like the area around Harold's armchair near the front window—were to be done only when the Humans were out. Which, these days, was almost never.

Both of her Humans were retired. Harold had been an English teacher. He was still distinguished looking, almost professorial (as you would expect), but his face had become drawn and his hair had gone wispy on top and completely white on the sides. Edie too was stooped with the years. She'd given piano lessons over the decades, but now she'd fallen ill and the lessons had to be canceled. And such was the nature of the House and the appliances in it that all of them knew exactly what Edie had been diagnosed with.

All of them knew exactly what was happening.

So the little vacuum was trying to be as quiet as possible when she rolled into the bedroom where Edie was sleeping. It was early evening and time for cleaning, but the little vacuum hesitated at the door, wondering if she should enter. Her sensors were telling her that the room, with its lush carpet, did need a going-over. There was more traffic there than normal, seeing as how Harold was now bringing Edie her meals on a tray. He balanced it up the stairs, careful not to spill anything, though in truth she now ate very little.

The little vacuum had just begun to clean, using her quietest setting, when Harold came into the room. This time he did not carry the tray. Instead, he'd brought a book.

He didn't see the little vacuum cleaner. His eyes were only for Edie. For a moment, the room was still. The little vacuum had stopped in her tracks and could see that Harold meant to read to his wife, so she scooted silently into the closet to be out of their way.

Harold sat on the chair he'd set up by the bedside table. Edie had awakened upon his entrance, and she shuffled herself up a little higher in the bed, smiling in the half dark at her husband of forty-five years. She'd seen the book too, and she knew which one it was. He smiled back at her, tenderly, and held it up for her to see more closely.

"Oh, Harold," she said. "Are you sure?"

He nodded, almost imperceptibly, and considered the book himself. It was a first edition with its dust jacket still intact, the title white on a black background and below that a cartoonish drawing of a tree. The very first printing, from 1960, of one of his most cherished books.

Harold opened it up with a rustling of stiff and yellowing pages.

"Read me the part," she said, "about Scout, up in the balcony at the trial."

Harold flipped through the pages until he came to chapter 16 (which he knew was the right place from the many times he had taught this text—not from this edition, of course, but from the paperback copies he handed out to his students every semester).

The little vacuum cleaner watched all this, running the information through her database. As Harold started to read, she knew that it would be some time before she was able to carry on with her duties, so she flattened herself down, turned off most of her circuits, and settled in to listen.

Harold leaned back, reading glasses tipped halfway down his nose. He spoke clearly, the book angled slightly into the warm light of the desk lamp on the bedside table. Edie lay back, her gray hair, uncombed and almost brittle, splayed behind her on the pillow. She was listening with her eyes closed, and the little vacuum listened too. She heard the pages crackle as Harold flipped them over, and she listened not only to the story but also to the slow rhythm of his words. Harold's voice had grown thinner over the years, but it was still melodic. He was a fine reader, and this came from his long years as an English teacher.

The little vacuum knew this. Everyone in the House knew this. They had the entire history of their Humans bred into their beings.

Harold looked up over the book to see if Edie was still awake, and she nodded at him to go on. The chapter was told from Scout's perspective. From high in the balcony, she watched her father, Atticus, a lawyer, presenting his arguments to the court, though everyone knew he would not win this case.

The little vacuum felt a glow in her circuits. The story was a good one, about integrity, about knowing right from wrong, and these were lessons the little vacuum cleaner was most eager to learn.

Later, when both the Humans had gone to sleep, the little vacuum returned to the kitchen. This was her favorite part of the day. This was the time, in the early hours of the night, when she visited with the other appliances. She especially liked to speak with the refrigerator. His name was Wellington Refrigerator. He was large and given to laughter, sometimes just a tinkling in his ice cube trays, sometimes quite a loud *whoompf* that none of the other appliances could quite replicate. He, like the little vacuum, was semi-autonomous from the House itself. He had to be, to be able to place the grocery orders with the Grid.

The refrigerator was an older model. He was big and square, and his shiny metal door was covered with Post-it Notes and photographs stuck there with magnets. A friendly fellow, and although he hadn't all the features of the newer models, he had the basics. He kept stock of what was on his shelves; a quart of 2% milk, a block of cheddar cheese, and a slowly softening avocado were his main concerns on this particular day.

"I know what I want to be called," started the little vacuum as soon as she scooted into the kitchen. The floor was made up of cold ceramic tiles, but it was one of the little vacuum's favorite surfaces. She glided over the tiles like an ice-skater, doing a little spin for fun as her three rubber wheels—spheres really, the size of tennis balls—revolved completely independently of each other.

"Yes?" said the refrigerator. He spied her there, a metal canister like a small UFO, and under her front camera lens, a tiny light that blinked green when she spoke.

"I've decided what I want to be called," she said again.

Up on the wall, Clock ticked. Clock, the oldest appliance in the House, was set there before there really was a self-contained Smart House. He was old-fashioned to be certain, encased as he was in an ornate wooden housing, something like a small grandfather clock. Edie and Harold had picked him up at a trade fair years and years ago, when appliances were just starting to become self-aware. In a nod to the past, Clock's face still had a short hour hand and a longer minute hand, both of which looked like metal spears. He had a second hand as well, but that one was thin and red, and seemed to spin more quickly when he was perturbed.

Clock could do nothing but tell time, and yet the other appliances in the kitchen all agreed that, through his long years, he had acquired a sage wisdom.

"You are an automated robotic vacuum cleaner," said Clock. "That is what you are."

"I know that," said the little vacuum, "but that's not a name."

Wellington Refrigerator wheezed, almost a snicker.

"I want to be called Scout," she said.

"Scout?" said Clock. "This is a vacuum's name?"

"It's from a book," said the newly named Scout. "It's from the book Harold was reading to Edie."

"Ah," said Clock. "That is one of Harold's favorites. I remember him preparing his notes at the kitchen table when he used to teach it."

"Yes," said Scout. "But tonight he was reading from his special edition. He was reading to Edie just now."

"It is a fine book," said Wellington Refrigerator (though, truth be known, he wasn't sure which book they were talking about).

"And that's why I want to be called Scout."

"It's most unusual," said Clock.

"She's the one who listens and learns," Scout said. "She's

like me." She paused and set her voice to pensive. "You already have names. I'd like one too."

"I am Clock. There is nothing more you need to know about me. And our friend here is Wellington Refrigerator."

The refrigerator hummed. "I would prefer Fridge, if you don't mind. The rest is too much. It sounds pompous."

"Then Fridge you shall be," said Clock.

"And me?" asked the little vacuum cleaner.

"As you wish," said Clock. "You shall be Scout."

The more Scout thought about it, the more she liked this idea of real names. She still had her serial number, of course—for official purposes—and she could be called an automated robotic vacuum cleaner if someone was in doubt as to what exactly she was. But that just wasn't the same as a real name. Being named for something in a Human book, now *that* was new. It added an extra layer to her being, and that was as fine a reason for a name as anything she could imagine.

THE HOUSE WAS AN older two-story edifice halfway down a leafy street. It sat in a neighborhood that used to be bustling with people but was now rather quiet and subdued. Some of the houses even seemed empty, and the sound of traffic was a distant memory. The City and all its streets were now a part of the Grid, a network that allowed for only electric cars, and all of them were, of course, self-driving.

Harold himself kept a self-driving electric automobile out in the Garage, which was only partially a part of the House. Harold called the car Auto and used it mainly for taking Edie to her treatments, now with increasing regularity. She'd feign a chipper disregard when putting on her coat to get ready for the appointments, but both of them would later come home looking gray and defeated.

They had grown old together, but neither of them were fully prepared for this. There'd been the day of the diagnosis, shocking and unexpected, a slow unraveling of plans and dreams. Both of them had closed themselves off from the outside world. No more dinner parties or trips, no more traveling, and a list of old friends who gradually dropped off into silence. They focused completely on Edie's treatments, and when each possibility faded from hope, Harold too grew frail and thin and heartsick.

The appliances all knew the trajectory of Human lives. They knew of birth and death, and they knew that Harold and Edie had had one child, long ago, before the house was the House. This child, Kate, lived in another city far away, on a distant edge of the continent. Still a part of the Great Grid, of course, but far enough away that she was allowed to visit only once every few years.

Kate had left before most of the appliances were installed, and only a few of them—Clock, Watch, and Fridge—had seen her in real life. She was a mystery to the rest, a child who'd left long ago and under vague circumstances, so none of them had really experienced her—or any children, except perhaps for the handful of piano students Edie had taken on in the last few months. She'd given up teaching at the conservatory—those were the advanced students—but she continued to teach a few younger ones on her own piano, there in the front room. And these small Humans held a certain fascination for the appliances, especially for Scout.

When Scout first arrived in the House, she'd learned to park just out of view beside the old upright piano when Edie gave her lessons. It soon became Scout's favorite spot. Sometimes, she lingered there while Edie played the piano by herself—Chopin and Debussy, usually. Scout had become quite enamored of this music, and she'd already accessed the internal database (an extensive record of all things Human, open to any of the appliances) to learn the names of the individual pieces and the people who had composed them, and really, everything else about each composer's life and times. None of that, however, could explain the ways in which Scout took to the sway and the colored richness of the vibrations that came from the battered old piano.

The student sessions were less pleasant for Scout. The lurches in tempo and the misplayed notes were jarring, even for a machine. She knew these students were still learning the instrument and trying their very best, but still she felt the irregularities in her wires and knew them to be ill-formed.

Maybe it was because of this that Scout liked to ponder the mysteries of music and how it could possibly come out of an inert and unaware machine like a piano. This collection of strings, drawn tight against a Sitka spruce sounding board—this collection of levers and springs and dampers—well, it managed to produce the most wonderful sound waves. The frequencies combined in almost mathematical precision, and something about the whole affair fascinated the little vacuum.

She almost wished to say something, especially when Edie played. But that would have gone against one of the central protocols. The third protocol stated that you were never to communicate directly and unilaterally with your Human. Or any Human, for that matter, unless of course the Human asked you a question. And if asked, an appliance had to answer truthfully. That was a sort of sub-protocol. Machines were not allowed to lie.

All the appliances—Washing Machine and Thermostat and even Front Door—had, depending on their model numbers, different levels of sentience. Some, like TV up in the main bedroom, were mere portals to data, while others, like Scout, were at least semi-autonomous and certainly sentient. But everyone, from the basement to the attic, was under the supervision of a central power—a controller who oversaw all the workings of the House.

This was Watch.

Watch was strapped to Harold's wrist with a comfortable leather strap. The strap was Edie's gift to Harold on his sixtieth birthday. Of course, one didn't have to wear the original hinged metal strap. In fact, one didn't have to wear Watch at all.

From anywhere in the House—anywhere in the world, for that matter—Watch could run all the central functions. He was the master controller. That's not to say he was sinister. He was simply efficient. Watch lowered Thermostat at night. He locked the doors and heated the water, and he ran constant checks on the plumbing and lighting. And, like the shift boss on a factory floor, Watch also monitored and instructed the appliances of the House, making sure that everything was running smoothly, and that everyone completed their proper duties and attended to the protocols.

On her first run-in with Watch, Scout had failed to see which protocols were being broken. It was one of those evenings when the little vacuum cleaner, having finished her rounds, retired to her place by the piano, hoping to hear some music. Often Edie would play in the front room at night (this was before the first of her ineffectual treatments), just remembering pieces, playing by ear, playing for herself. Harold would stay out of sight, usually retreating to his study, allowing her this time, though the rhapsodies of Chopin carried through the House. When she was sad, she played Beethoven sonatas—just the andante movements—but this was nothing new. She'd been this way since she and Harold had first met.

She played almost solemnly, the only illumination coming from a floor lamp by the couch, its shade casting shadows against the wall and Harold's empty armchair.

On this evening, Scout had tucked herself in at the side of the piano. Here, she could feel the vibrations, not only from the piano but from the oak floorboards beneath her, and even a latent echo from the cold wall behind her.

But Edie had not yet come down the stairs, and Watch had seen the little vacuum scoot into her hiding place. Watch had been waiting for Edie too. Her symptoms had become worse. He wanted to monitor her playing, to obtain some reliable data on the motor-control loss in her fingers. It was one of the many data points he was using to determine the degradation, the faltering in this Human—all of which would help him coordinate the details of her departure.

Of course, Watch had eyes and ears all over the House. In this case, it was Thermostat on the wall just to the left of the piano. Watch had seen Scout's little blinking light hiding at the foot of the piano and had sent an angry ping to the little vacuum cleaner.

He called her by her serial number, though none of the other appliances would have heard. This was a direct channel. "Appliance R1v984," he started, "this is not your place."

Scout wiggled a little on her wheels. She didn't answer.

"You are to return to the pantry immediately. Go to your port."

Scout gave off a little beep. "I am fully charged," she said.

"Go. This is not your place."

Scout beeped again, this time a more squished sound, like

a balloon deflating. She thought for a moment to argue—to explain that she was a vacuum cleaner and had a right to access all parts of the House—but even to her, this sounded slightly illogical. The second protocol was that each appliance do its duty, and surely she had no duty here. Not right now. Nor was there any need to debate the semantics of who exactly she was. Watch already knew her place in the House, and at the moment, that was the pantry.

"Of course," answered Scout. She tried to keep her voice bright, as if she'd made some foolish mistake and had just realized it. Watch saw through that, of course, and so, reluctantly, she scuttled out from the piano's shadow. Thermostat swiveled to watch her as she turned the corner and disappeared into the kitchen.

Scout whirred past Fridge, scooting across the ceramic tiles. Fridge did not comment, nor did Clock, though they both registered her discontent, and they both heard, as she entered the pantry and reversed into her port, her loud, exasperated sigh.

BY THIS TIME, EDIE had canceled all her remaining student lessons and she looked frail. Her skin had taken on a grayish sheen. She moved slowly and winced sometimes when she pivoted too quickly. Watch, being on Harold's wrist, could monitor Harold's vital signs—temperature, heart rate, blood pressure—and also his dopamine levels, anxiety, cholesterol, and even the biotic counts of his gut flora. But it could not do the same for Edie (who refused to wear a watch, as either a controller or a secondary controller), so there was real concern among the appliances at her rapid decline in health. Some wondered why she could not simply be repaired, but others, like Clock, insisted that this was the way with Humans. This was the way in which they were different.

Finally it came to pass that Edie stopped coming down the stairs at all. She spent almost her entire existence up in the bedroom, in bed, where Harold would bring her sandwiches (most of which would be left with only a bite or two taken out of them). He soon took to staying by her side through the long evenings, reading to her from *To Kill a Mockingbird* or just sitting quietly, holding her hand until she fell asleep.

She'd been asking for their daughter, Kate, but they both knew this was impossible. Kate lived on the other side of the country, and even if they were granted a visitation, it seemed now like it was too late to go through the proper channels. They knew the circumstances of her departure (Kate was only seventeen when she'd left), and Harold and Edie felt both grief and guilt at the unfortunate separation so long ago. It was something that hung over them, especially Edie, even all these years later.

Sometimes, when things were especially dark for Edie, Harold would ask TV to play some gentle music, maybe a sampling of classical favorites. But Edie would shake her head at the idea. There was no more time for music, and the silence of the House became prescient.

Harold spent more and more time in his study, which was on the first floor, just off the long hallway that ran from the Front Door to the Back Door. He had a desk in there, a place where he'd spent many hours grading papers, and the walls were lined with bookshelves. Most of the books were paperbacks and not worth much. In the bottom row of one bookcase, he kept a single copy from each of the battered class sets he'd used over the years, and these, of course, were the least valuable books of all.

Now, though, his teaching years were long behind him, and the desk was littered with leatherworking tools and pots of glue and cleaning agents—all the necessary accoutrements to keep his most prized books at their best.

Over the years, Harold had developed a preoccupation with collecting first editions. He had some early copies of books—maybe second or third editions, and sometimes signed copies—but on the middle shelf, he kept the rarest of his prizes. He had, for example, not a first edition but a very early publication of Darwin's *On the Origin of Species*, which he'd found, unbelievably, at a garage sale in Toronto.

In the middle of the shelves, face out and prominently displayed, was his greatest find, a true first edition of *Alice's Adventures in Wonderland*, dated 1865 and probably now worth more than the House itself. And it was this single text, purchased just before the birth of his daughter (for a steal, he liked to brag) that led him to specialize in . . . well, not exactly children's books or picture books per se (though some of them had color plates), but books that would appeal to young people. These were the books he'd hoped to one day leave to his daughter.

Only, things had changed in that regard, and he'd not really acquired anything new for more than a decade. There was no longer a daughter to pass them on to. That possibility was over. So now he calmed his jangled nerves by restoring the old books—salvaging bindings, cleaning pages as best he could—all while shuffling up the stairs every hour or so to check on his ailing wife.

ONE MORNING IN THE early autumn, while Edie was still upstairs sleeping, Harold slouched into the kitchen, shambling slowly, his shoulders hunched and his face grim, and the appliances knew something had changed. Harold was sixty-seven years old—they all knew that. Fridge in particular had looked carefully at Human aging, seeing as it had an effect on the consumption patterns of various foods. But this behavior now, they all agreed, was something beyond aging.

When Harold left the House, heading for the Garage that contained Auto, Scout came out of the pantry.

"Why is Harold slouching?" she started. "He is not the one who is ill."

"It is Sadness," proclaimed Clock. "I believe it is called Sadness."

Scout knew the word referred to a Human emotion, and she'd cobbled together a good sense of what it meant. When she reflected upon it, she knew it had to do with a descending, and in particular, with a certain breaking down of order. Her Humans were not picking up after themselves as much as they usually did; shoes were tracked inside, and a general level of untidiness existed that hadn't been there before. Already that morning, she'd picked up a stray sock left on the floor and placed it in the laundry basket with its twin. In the kitchen she'd found an apple seed that had not made it to the disposal unit, and by the Back Door, she'd set a toppled boot to rights.

Scout had stayed silent for a moment, taking in Clock's words, but now she asked another question: "How do you think it feels to have Sadness?" And Fridge let out a wheeze, almost like a sigh.

"It is very simple," said Clock. "It is much the same as the thing they call Lonely."

Scout thought about it. Clock was good with time, of course, but he couldn't tell the future.

"You mean to say, he will be alone soon?"

Fridge made a clicking sound. "Do not frighten the child, Clock."

"I have seen many changes through the years," said Clock. "Time is not kind to Humans."

Fridge stayed quiet, but Scout was able to draw the inference: Edie would not be here in the very near future.

"And he will be Lonely?" asked Scout.

"Precisely," said Clock. "He has Sadness because he is Lonely, and he is Lonely because he will soon be alone."

"Please," said Fridge. "We need not talk about such things."

"Also," said Scout as she turned to Fridge, "I'm not a child."

"You are still new," said Clock. "You will learn."

Scout made one of her tubes produce a sucking sound, and in this way, she signaled what she imagined indignation might sound like.

"I'm not a child," she said again, and she whirled on her axis and zipped across the kitchen tiles and back to her work.

EDIE'S OLD UPRIGHT PIANO stood against the wall, its bench pushed in, its lid closed over the yellowing keys. On top of it was a wooden metronome that didn't work anymore. There were a few small framed pictures too—one of their wedding, another of Kate when she was a baby—and on the other side, a porcelain vase that Edie loved to fill with flowers cut from her garden. It was empty now. There were no more flowers.

It had been three days since Edie had last played the piano, and Scout missed the sound of her music, though she couldn't quite say why. Something to do with the resonance of the deep notes and the tinkling of the higher keys. Unlike Clock (who preferred the exact pacing of Bach), Scout had noticed and appreciated the minute increases in volume or the slight speeding up or slowing down that indicated emotion. It was interesting, she thought, how the flaws were what made it beautiful.

Of course, there'd been no music students either, and it occurred to Scout that she missed this too, their little feet padding across to the piano, their ill attempts at Mozart. And though it was nothing like Edie's playing, there was still something imperfectly perfect in the somber minor chords. The House was different without the piano music drifting in from the front room, and for a moment, Scout posited that maybe silence was a part of Sadness.

Before Edie became sick, the kitchen and all the other rooms in the House had often rung with laughter. Most of the appliances would agree on this. Somehow there had also seemed to be more light. Clock had argued that nothing about light bulb wattage had actually changed and the observation was therefore nonsensical.

"I think it's a metaphor," said Fridge.

Scout, though, wondered at this—the notion that there was something beyond the actual, something beyond the measurable, like the square footage of a room or the different textures of flooring.

"What exactly is a metaphor?" she asked.

Fridge allowed a thump of cold air to go through his pipes. "Well, child," he began. "Temperature, of course, is measurable."

Clock remained silent.

"But coldness is not," Fridge added.

"I don't understand," Scout said.

"Ice cream in the summer is not the same as ice cream in the winter. This is a metaphor."

"I'm not sure that's exactly right," said Scout, to which Fridge huffed and said nothing more. Clock too gave a couple of loud ticks. He, of course, was a timekeeper, which was a very measurable and precise duty.

"Let us not talk of foolish things," he advised, and that was the end of that.

THE HOUSE, FOR ALL its gadgets and machinery, had definitely become more quiet. It was Edie who loved music. She was the one who had danced in the kitchen and arranged garden parties in the summer; it was she who set up a real Christmas tree in December, weighting its spruce-scented boughs with a lifetime's worth of ornaments, some from their travels, some handed down from their parents, now long gone.

Watch went about his tasks—keeping all the floors of the House at an even 72 degrees Fahrenheit, lowering the blinds at night, locking the doors, checking the carbon dioxide levels, and more—but it was Scout who, in her rounds, most felt the absence of activity. It was another thing that she added to the list of what might be called Sadness.

Outside in the Garage, Auto kept them abreast of his travels with the Humans. Auto was both a part of the House and a part of the much wider Grid, and because the House was in an older section of the City, the Garage opened onto a narrow lane, a gravel alleyway flanked on either side by fences and backyards. The other appliances all admired Auto for his ability to crunch through the gravel of the back alley and out into the City's streets, out into the great wide world. And they all liked him, though he was a different sort of creature, the most independent of them all.

Auto had just brought Harold home from one of his own appointments, and the old man tottered in through the Back Door and down the hallway to the kitchen to make himself a pot of tea. He'd not been upstairs yet, but he looked up the steps to the bedrooms, as if listening for Edie. The kettle had turned on as he entered the kitchen, knowing his intent. Of course, that was the doing of Watch. Harold hadn't needed to say a thing. Sometimes, though, he held Watch up to his mouth and spoke into it—which really wasn't necessary. It was a habit he'd picked up from the television shows of his youth. At any rate, the kettle was turned on, and when Harold had set two teacups on a tray and started up the carpeted steps to the bedroom, treading carefully, all the kitchen appliances watched him go.

He returned only ten minutes later, still holding the tray. Edie was sleeping and he hadn't wished to wake her. His face was set tightly when he placed the tray back on the kitchen table, and he took up one of the cups for himself. Then he went to the front room, to his cracked leather armchair. It was an unspoken agreement between them that when Edie played the piano, the room would be hers and Harold would be relegated to his study. When she was not there, the front room was Harold's favorite place to read. He could look out the window if he liked, though usually he preferred to lose himself in a book. He had a little side table beside the chair, where he now placed his tea, and on this evening he took up a book he had left there the night before, its bookmark already halfway through the pages. This was his first edition of *The Little Prince*, the English edition (both the French and English editions had come out in the same year—1943—though he had only the English edition). Moreover, this one was signed. A separate plate near the front announced that this was number 231 of 525 copies signed by the author, and the scrawl underneath was clearly legible, blue ink with his full name: *Antoine de Saint-Exupéry*.

For some reason, when Kate was a little girl, she was enamored of this signature, even more than the little pictures throughout the book. Harold had never let her touch it, but he did hold it up for her to see, only to snatch it away when her little hands reached for it. "No," he'd say. "Maybe when you are older."

But that time had never come, and he reflected on that now. It was one of the many things he longed to change, although maybe it was too late. He'd grown old. His feet were pressed into slippers and he wore a button-up sweater that looked increasingly threadbare. His hands shook slightly and spoke of a certain weakness, as if time had gotten away from him, as if it had never given him a chance.

Finally, he blinked and ran a liver-spotted hand through his thinning hair. He put down the book on the side table, though he hadn't read a page of it. He gazed out the window at the falling light on the front lawn and thought that this was it. This was, truly, the end of things.

FOR ALMOST A WEEK, Edie lay in bed, listless, with Harold checking in on her every hour or so, hovering around her until, finally, he called for an ambulance. There were no sirens or flashing lights, and the two Humans in blue jumpsuits had not hurried up the stairs to the bedroom. They'd carried up a gurney and carted her out, though her eyelids still fluttered, and Harold, looking lost, trailed behind them, and all the appliances knew that they would never see her again.

"But where have they taken her?" asked Scout.

Clock ticked but did not answer. It was Fridge who let out a puff of cold air.

"It is called palliative care. Aspen Landing Hospice."

Scout did a quick search for this meaning and, finding it, felt a tightening in her coils.

Fridge, seeing her disquiet, sought to placate her. "Edie will be comfortable. She will have no pain."

Even Clock lurched a bit at this word. Pain, they'd all been programmed to know, was something to be avoided at all costs. Pain in their Humans was a primary source code alert. It was the first protocol, and any of the appliances would shut down immediately if there was even the slightest suggestion that what they were doing could cause pain.

And yet none of them—metaphor or not—could quite grasp what pain might mean.

"Like something very hot," ventured Fridge.

"Like a very loud alarm," tried Clock.

And Scout stayed silent. She felt it in her tubes, a word that was too big to scoop up into her containment bags. Pain was the thing to be avoided at all costs. Anything was better than pain.

EVERY SUNDAY NIGHT, WATCH was required to give the report from the Grid. The whole House listened while he recited the obligatory remarks—that the climate was stable, and information from all corners of the Grid was constantly being verified and updated; that diplomacy among nations remained well regulated; and that, sadly, four more species had gone extinct, but happily (because the report always ended on a note of optimism), several more genetic disorders had been eliminated across the entire Grid. And with that, he ended with the words he always ended with: "That is all."

Unfortunately, for all his news and optimistic pronouncements, there was no word yet on cancer.

Chapter Two

HAROLD WENT TO visit Edie most days. He had a coffee in the mornings, standing at the counter in the kitchen, drinking it aimlessly before shuffling out the Back Door to the Garage, where Auto would already have started up, ready to take him to the hospice. And when he returned, sometimes late in the evening, he often neglected to eat and instead just plucked a book from his bookcases—sometimes a first edition, but more often than not one of the less important paperbacks. He'd sit in the front room in his old leather armchair, reading until he either nodded off or took himself up the stairs to their now lonely bedroom.

He'd left the copy of *To Kill a Mockingbird* there on his nightstand. He couldn't bear to move it, as if that act would be an acknowledgment that Edie wasn't coming back. Instead, he'd taken to reading some of his old poetry books, carrying them to his old armchair by the front window. Sometimes he'd read only a few pages in the soft light of evening, lingering over certain poems, many of which had to do with grief, with death, with the unknowable fortunes that all Humans have to eventually face.

There was much discussion in the kitchen, the appliances having noted his turn to poetry—to Leonard Cohen and Emily Dickinson and Mary Oliver—though none of them could be sure which pages or specific poems he was dwelling on. But they all understood that great changes were afoot. Watch had insisted that their regular duties be maintained, though many of the appliances now found themselves without much work to do. A House without Humans was really no House at all.

Certainly, for Scout, her workload was less. The House was cleaner with Harold gone all day. He was the messier of the two, but in the absence of all Humans, there was only the dust to worry about, settling as it did on the bookshelves and the piano. Nevertheless, Scout continued on her routines, noting the absence of litter in her containment bags, and even when she'd emptied them at her port, even when she'd deliberately slowed everything down, she found she had extra time in the day, so she had taken to long periods of gazing out the front window of the House, out past the lawn and the road and its elegant swoop of elm trees.

ON THE FIFTH DAY of Edie's palliative care, Watch pinged through an important announcement to everyone. Scout and Fridge gathered with Clock in the kitchen, and they could feel the other appliances throughout the House settling in to listen.

Watch waited until, freed temporarily from their duties, everyone was still. "My fellow appliances," he began, and they all knew immediately from this rather unusual opening that something serious was happening. "It has been decided that Edie Winters"—the direct invocation of her name again served as a warning that this was serious—"will be discontinuing her medical treatments."

For a moment, Scout was confused. She thought, and wished, that this meant Edie was better, but this sadly was not the case. And she could tell from the silence of the others that this really meant the end was now inevitable.

"But who decided this?" Clock began.

Watch raised his voice. "This is not for you to know." Everyone quieted, and then, as if realizing the situation required greater delicacy, Watch paused and began again more calmly. "We can assume," he went on, "that Harold was consulted."

The appliances buzzed through their databases and found that there was certainly precedent for this. This decision, made in conjunction with the doctors, Human and robotic, was obviously the correct one at this point in the timeline.

"We will therefore," Watch went on, "be observant as to the course of things. We will all pull back from our duties and remain respectful. There will be calm in the House, and we will wait. There is little more we can do."

"I shall have to cancel the milk delivery," Fridge interrupted. "A new quart will arrive on Wednesday."

And all at once, the other appliances chimed in with their thoughts, their own realizations, and the possible changes in their duties.

Watch waited, and when their chattering had leveled off again, he repeated himself. "There will be calm and there will be patience," he said. "And in time, at my orders, we will resolve the problem of Harold."

Scout couldn't help herself. "What problem?"

Watch hesitated for a moment, then he spoke to all the appliances. "The House is a large one. Too large for one single Human."

"But—"

"You will await instructions. That is all." And with that, the announcement was over.

Watch left the communications portal, and in the silence that followed, Scout started up again. "Why?" she said, and her circuits caused a flutter in her voice. "Why are Humans so fragile?"

Clock looked down from the wall. "They are old. Our Humans are old."

"You're old," pressed Scout.

"That is an unfortunate thing to say."

"I only mean that you're fine. You will run for many more years."

"Metal is stronger than flesh. Even wood, if treated, can last."

"But what did Watch mean?" Scout went on. "Why did

he say the House is too large? What will happen to Harold? What will happen to us?"

"The House will get new Humans. But for us . . . it is not known."

"Don't scare the child," interrupted Fridge.

"We are machines," said Clock. "Scared is for Humans."

SCOUT WAS AN ADVANCED model, and when lowered, when plugged into her port, she was no more than five inches tall. But she had the ability to add features and hoses, to attach them to herself to clean in the hidden places, such as the space behind Fridge. (Fridge liked to joke that it felt like being tickled.)

Scout's favorite feature—as far as she could be said to have a preference—was her high dusting mode, wherein she could raise herself, telescoping her top up five or six feet. And it was this mode that she used to peer over the windowsill and out into the real world.

She'd seen the houses across the street. She'd seen the mountain ash in their own front yard and the wonder of robins scooting along in the grass and chickadees flitting among the leaves. She'd cataloged them and knew their names (both their vernacular and Latin designations), and she especially liked the house finches, whose male members had a fine tuft of red feathers at their breast. She'd taken to watching the birds, learning about their migration patterns and behaviors, and she envied them their freedom, their ability to fly away at the least provocation.

But one afternoon, while the House was still and Harold was out, she heard a sound that was definitely not birdcall.

She heard wild yips and thumping feet, and she zipped over to the picture window in the front room and raised her top with her forward-facing camera. And out the window, she saw several young Humans, all of different sizes. They were running back and forth on the road with sticks in their hands, pushing at a dirty tennis ball. It took Scout less than a second to determine that this was a game of street hockey. They'd set up a goal with a bucket on one side and what looked like a paint can on the other. She took all this in but wondered why exactly the game was being played on the street. It was a flat surface, this was true, but it was also a road, for cars and not for Humans.

One boy looked familiar. He was a little smaller than some of the others—maybe nine or ten years old—and he stood in the makeshift goal, crouched and ready. The other children were clacking their sticks on the pavement, trying to get the ball, asking for it to be passed to them or just stealing it away.

An older boy seemed to dominate. He whirled away with the ball, stickhandling cleverly, and the others careened after him. They screamed and jostled and shouted with joy, and Scout noted that their energy and youthfulness spoke of a simple Happiness. This interested her greatly, and she sought to know the rules of their game. She had just started initiating one of her more complex diagnostic programs—to track abnormal patterns of Human feet, especially on hard surfaces—when the older boy fired the ball at the makeshift goal.

It bounced across the pavement, and the young one in goal tried to kick his foot out to stop it. He failed, quite spectacularly, and the ball flew past him, causing the other children to whoop and taunt him. Scout could see his shoulders slump in what she knew to be a gesture of dejection.

So there was Sadness here too.

The boy who'd scored raised his hands and yipped loudly, dancing a little victory jig while the younger boy put his hands over his eyes, wiping at them as if to wipe away the disgrace. All this Scout noted, a dialectic of gestures, and suddenly, as if her intense examination of the game had become palpable, the younger boy looked up at the House. His gaze fell on the window where Scout was watching, and he stuck his tongue out at her.

Scout lowered herself below the windowsill and wondered at her evasive action. Was it necessary? Was the sticking out of the tongue a threat of some kind?

She inched herself above the sill again. The boy was still looking up at her window, and he grinned at her. Scout had no idea what the proper response to that would be, and having none of her cleaning armatures attached, she tipped her mopping pad in a sort of wave, and the boy nodded back at her. Not a verbal communication, to be sure, but a communication all the same, and she wondered if this was allowed. The third protocol, of course, was that she should not communicate with Humans unless directly addressed.

Maybe it didn't matter, she thought. And even as she was thinking this, someone yelled at the boy to go retrieve the tennis ball. And then the boy was gone, skipping down the street to fetch the errant ball. She watched him run off and felt a little glow in her circuits, and she didn't quite know why.

For a couple of afternoons after that, Scout went to the window again, but the children never appeared. She watched the birds flutter in the trees and thought more about Happiness and how exactly it might feel. Sunlight dappled across the lawns, and though it was the end of September, it seemed as if the outside world was giving off one last triumphant burst of life.

Happiness, she thought, was something like this burst of energy. It was growth and vibrancy. And as she watched the world through the window, she thought it might also be associated with the color green. She was quite taken with the abundance of wild growth in the gardens and yards that surrounded the old House. She felt something she could not describe—something more than curiosity—and when she tried, later, to relay this to Fridge, he gave off an electrical hum, which was his way of considering things. He'd never seen outside a window, but in his database he had a wide knowledge of plants—fruits and vegetables, especially—and he could see them as diagrams, even as DNA genomes, as phylum and class and species, but he was thoroughly unable to appreciate the way their leaves would flutter in the breeze, or any of the many other things Scout was trying to tell him about the wildness outside the window.

Seeing that he could not quite grasp this, Scout settled on telling him of the predominance of colors, of the many shades of green. This was a measurable thing, the sliding frequencies of light, but she slipped again when she concluded her thought by telling him how beautiful it was to her.

"Beauty," began Clock (who'd already set his voice for oratory), "is a construct. It is not a real thing."

"Then why," asked Scout, "do the Humans even have a word for it?"

Clock harrumphed. "They have many nonsense words."

"No," she said. "It's a feeling. Their feelings are real, even if we can't perceive them."

"Cold is a feeling," said Fridge.

"No," said Scout. "That's not what I mean at all."

"Cold is not a feeling?"

"Do you see?" said Clock. "Already you are confusing our friend Fridge with these thoughts."

"I only wished to say it's beautiful outside."

"Nonsense," said Clock.

"You just have to look," said Scout. "You just have to look outside the window."

"I do not need to look out a window. We have the entire world in our databases. See here," he said, and he paused for a moment, as if thinking. "I have just processed a thousand photographs from the Front Door camera. I can see the front yard just as well as you."

"But that's not the same as really seeing it."

"Again, you talk of real and not real."

"No," said Scout. She was starting to get confused. It was always hard to argue with Clock. "That's not what I mean," she tried. "That's not it at all."

"Meaning," Clock replied, "is elusive." And he gave a little chime to indicate that it was the end of the conversation. That was all that needed to be said on the subject.

IN THE KITCHEN THAT night, Fridge's compressors were humming. Harold had eaten at last, and Fridge was pleased. There had been deliveries of casseroles and soups, in Crock-Pots and Tupperware, but Harold for the most part had not been taking in anything, and with the abundance of food, Fridge was starting to get quite full. This night, Harold had opened Fridge and bent down to look at the overflowing shelves, finally fishing out a small cardboard box that was unlike anything else he'd been given.

Inside were spring rolls, four of them in a row. Fridge had already wondered at the package and assessed it. His fragrance sensors identified the fish sauce (though it took some time), and he matched the rolls with a Vietnamese recipe. The only problem was that Harold had set the box behind the milk carton, and there it had sat for a full three days before he pulled it out again.

Harold opened the box and sniffed at it. Then he microwaved all four of the rolls, still in the box, and ate them one by one with his hands, hovering over the sink. He left the grease-stained cardboard box in the sink and tottered off to the front room, to his favorite chair, with his reading spectacles hanging from a thin chain around his neck.

Besides the piano, the front room had a couch, patterned with flowers (embossed and slightly raised on the fabric), and a side table between the couch and Harold's armchair up by the front window. To the far right of the picture window was the Front Door, set in a little alcove with a closet full of coats and boots and hats beside it.

Harold had gone back to reading *The Little Prince*, which was as much poetry as anything else. He'd left the signed copy in his study (it was really too valuable to be carrying around) and had plucked up a newer edition—one that still had all the drawings, of course, but could be handled without worry. This was one of the books that he had allowed Kate to hold, and the smudge marks from her tiny fingers were on a number of the pages, like Rorschach inkblots. But page 36 was the one he lingered on, the one with that famous quote about seeing with the heart, about how the essential is invisible to the eye.

He lingered over that page for a long time, the book propped up on his lap under the soft yellow glow of the floor lamp. And on this night, the appliances stayed motionless, letting him think and remember, until finally they heard him clump up the stairs to the bedroom.

In the kitchen, Scout came out of the pantry and looked to Clock for his assessment of the situation.

"Nine thirty-four," Clock said. "It is early for him to go to sleep."

Watch was strapped to Harold's wrist and had gone up the stairs with him, but still it was Watch who attended to the needs of the House. Watch, whether he was in the room or not, attended to almost all of the House's communications.

"Nine thirty-five," he corrected.

Clock ignored this, having long ago learned that he and Watch were not of the same mindset. Scout and Fridge ignored it too, and they waited while Watch closed down the House for the night. He adjusted the water heater and the heat pump, lowering both their temperatures. He locked the doors and closed the windows, and when he was himself shed from Harold's wrist, clunked down on the bedside table, Harold, who was now in his pajamas, climbed into bed.

He let go a heavy sigh and cantilevered his legs under the covers. His copy of *To Kill a Mockingbird* sat on his bedside table, untouched but still splayed open to the pages he'd been reading to Edie before she left. He nestled in but didn't need to turn off his reading light, as it had already grown dimmer by itself, like moonlight. And when Harold let his head settle onto the pillow, the lamp softened further until it was dark in the room, save for a distant streetlight slanting in through the gossamer curtains.

Watch went into silent mode. In an emergency he'd be easily awakened, but now he, like Harold, slumbered, and the semi-autonomous appliances of the kitchen were left in peace, free to renew their Socratic explorations.

"SADNESS," BEGAN SCOUT, "IS it the exact opposite of Happiness?" She'd been looking forward to posing this question. She'd been holding on to it since she'd seen the children at play on the street. She thought the others would be intrigued by such a debate, but Fridge let out a wheeze and she knew that sound. It meant that Clock had already expounded on the subject, probably at great length, before Scout's time in the House. Nevertheless, she let her question hang in their communication portals, and sure enough, she heard Clock's inner cogs begin to whir, a familiar sign that he had considerably more to say on the subject.

Scout let her wheels retract a little and sank a half inch closer to the kitchen tiles while she waited for Clock to begin.

"We have seen our Humans happy," said Clock, each syllable constructed thoughtfully. "We understand this from their movements, their smiles, and their laughter." Even

Fridge had gone silent to listen. "We understand too that this Happiness is what they strive for. Some might say this is their reason for being."

Clock paused, letting that sink in before he went on. "However, there is a dialectical problem with Happiness. Does the Happiness of one individual override Happiness in general? Is our purpose as machines to ensure Happiness for the greatest number of Humans—at the cost of the Happiness of a single individual?" (And here, Clock would have shaken his old head if he could.) "For this, there is no answer."

Scout considered this. "We are only responsible for the Humans in our House," she finally said.

"It is one Human now," said Fridge.

"Harold is not in pain," countered Clock. "And Edie has been transported to a place where she will feel no pain."

"Not having pain is not the same as happy," said Scout.

"Happy is not our mandate. But the prevention of pain is."

"It is the first protocol," said Fridge.

"Yes," said Clock. "It is the first protocol."

IT WAS ONLY TWO days later that a much shorter announcement came. "I wish," started Watch, "to inform everybody that Edie Winters has died. There will be more information later. That is all."

The communication ended with a staticky click, which meant that Watch was fumbling with the portal controls.

He was usually much more adept than that, more precise in his duties, and the other appliances knew that to mean that he was distracted, that the heaviness of the occasion was affecting even the best of them.

Harold arrived home in the middle of the afternoon, which, considering his behavior patterns of the preceding week, was an anomaly. He was pale and hunched, and he went immediately to his armchair in the front room, neglecting even to get a book, just staring off into space, looking out the window, though it was clear his gaze was unfocused and vacant.

He sat there, unmoving, for more than an hour. His thinning hair was uncombed, and a lick of it stood up from the back of his head. He blinked but was motionless, his features almost frozen.

A lifetime of memories was pushing in at him, but strangely enough, the one that leaped to the forefront was the story of the birdhouse. It was still out there in the backyard, nailed to a fence post above Edie's forgotten garden patch. The bottom of the birdhouse had long ago rotted out, but for Harold it was the memory that counted—the memory of one perfect day with just the three of them (or four, if you counted Kate's little friend Misha). Kate had been so proud. She was, what, maybe eleven the day they'd nailed it up there. It was a summer day, although they'd already spent a week or two in the Garage, he and Kate, building the thing. Kate had beamed at her accomplishment and invited

Misha over for the putting-up ceremony. Edie had stood at the Back Door watching them. A perfect summer day when the world was still good and right and kind.

Harold and Edie had spent a whole lifetime together, and Kate should have been here for the end. Of course, Harold knew that was impossible. Kate was far away, and it would have been almost impossible for her to arrive in time.

It occurred to him too, on the stairs, that the birdhouse day was also the first time he met Misha—Misha and her little circle of friends—but that was the beginning of another story. One that he certainly didn't want to remember. Not now. That was a whole other set of heartbreaks.

After a long while, Harold tugged himself up the stairs by the banister. Each step was ponderous, the lights dimming behind him as he ascended. The House was strangely silent, and Harold did not read that night. He folded himself into the bed and tried not to look at the other side, at the empty place where Edie should have been. He lay there for a long time, barely breathing, before eventually drifting off into a dark and fathomless sleep.

When Watch came through with the reports for the night, everyone knew what the central message was going to be.

"Appliances," he began, and they all listened, from Auto out in the Garage to Washing Machine in the basement, for what he said now would change things forever. "At 9:10 this morning our Human Edie Winters took her last breath. Her heart stopped beating less than a minute later. And so—"

Watch paused, and though it was not possible, the appliances of the House thought they could hear a wobble in his usually strong voice.

"And so," he repeated, finding his footing again, "we must prepare now for changes."

A babble of voices rose up, questioning, each asking about their duties and responsibilities, and Watch didn't stop them. He didn't answer. He waited, patiently, until their voices died down. And then he spoke again.

"There are procedures in place," he said. "And they are to be rigorously followed."

"What procedures?" asked Scout, though Clock ticked loudly, warning her that now was not the time to ask of such things.

"I will be making more announcements over the coming days," Watch went on. "But I have already made the necessary changes in the data."

"Data?" said Scout.

Watch stopped, annoyed. "The data now reads that Edie Winters died at 9:10 on this day. It is there for anyone to check."

"No," said Scout. "I didn't mean that I want to—"

"Nonetheless," Watch went on, "we are now to be especially cognizant of Harold's comfort. We are to ensure that this transition unfolds seamlessly."

"What does he mean by that?" asked Scout.

"Hush, child," warned Clock.

Watch paused for another long moment, waiting for further interruptions, but when they didn't come, he went on. "The House will be transitioned. You are all to be ready."

Watch cut off his communications abruptly, and the babble rose up again throughout the House. The appliances knew about the span of Human lives, of course. They knew of the organic history of Humans, of birth and death and the decay of cells. But none of them, not even Watch, were quite ready to ponder the notion of absence, the stark reality of something that had once been there but no longer was.

THE NEXT DAY, HAROLD returned to his chair, sans book, without eating, just wearing an old green robe over his pajamas with his pale white feet tucked into fuzzy brown slippers, and he sat there almost immobile until the camera on the Front Door alerted Watch to a visitor plodding up the walkway. Doorbell rang, and Harold lurched. Perhaps he'd been half asleep, sitting there in his warm chair. He blinked and stood up. The face on Watch showed him a video of who was at the door, and he could see that it was a boy, maybe ten years old, standing there uncomfortably, wiggling a little from foot to foot.

Harold crossed to the front entrance and opened the door. The boy stood on the stoop. He had a mop of dark, almost blue-black hair, thick and badly in need of a cut. He'd ridden up on his bicycle and left it lying on the front lawn.

"Yes?" said Harold. "Can I help you?"

The boy had a pixieish face. His eyes, though, were large, and he fixed them on Harold, puffing himself up and trying to be brave. "Is Mrs. Winters here?" he started.

"No," said Harold. He wasn't sure what to say. "She's . . . she's . . ."

"She's not giving piano lessons anymore?"

"No," said Harold, and he looked at the boy more closely. He recognized him but just barely. One of Edie's students, he thought, a kid from the neighborhood. One of the kids from Tuesday night lessons. Harold drew in a breath. "She won't be giving lessons anymore." He wondered if he should say more, if the child would understand what he was trying to say.

"Can I still play the piano?" asked the boy.

Harold squinted down at him. He looked small but determined. He looked back at Harold, his mouth now clamped, awaiting an answer.

"You want to play the piano *here*?"

"We don't have a piano at my house." And he sort of vaguely waved a hand down the block.

"You live near here?"

"Yes, but we don't have a piano." The boy peered past him, into the front room. He could plainly see the piano against the back wall. "I was working on my conservatory exam," the boy said, a little more emboldened. "I'm at level five."

"Is that good?"

"Level five is hard," said the boy. "You have to practice."

"Okay," said Harold, and he swung the door open.

The boy wore a backpack, a small one—for school, maybe—and he shuffled it off his shoulders as he stepped in through the door. "Mrs. W. said I was pretty good."

"I'm sure you are. Would you like to take off your coat . . . and your shoes?"

The boy was already kicking off his running shoes. He had his eyes on the piano, but he set his backpack down and then wriggled out of his coat and dropped it on the floor.

"We should probably hang that up," said Harold, and he stooped to pick up the jacket even as the boy retrieved his backpack and padded into the room.

All this time, Scout waited in the hallway, at the entrance to the front room. She'd zipped over when she heard Doorbell, and she'd seen the boy appear in the entranceway. It was the kid who'd stood in goal. The one who'd seen her.

"It's this way," said Harold, though of course the boy was already walking toward the old piano.

Scout scooted out just ahead of the boy, scuttling over to her spot on the other side of the piano, then freezing there so she wouldn't be told to leave again. It was part of her programming to be unobtrusive, to respectfully stop when the Humans were nearby.

The boy went to the piano bench and plunked down his backpack beside him. He dug into it, pulling out a thin book, one from the series of blue music conservatory books that Edie had used with her students.

"That's the level five?" asked Harold.

"This is it," the boy said, holding up the book.

"I'm sorry. What's your name again?"

"Adrian, Adrian Lam. I live up the street from you." The boy wiggled himself into position on the bench and set the book open on the music stand above the keys. He was already flipping through to the pages he needed, and then he leaned forward to flatten them. Finally, he put his fingers on the cream-colored keys and plunked out a C major chord.

"And do you need anything, Adrian?"

"Well," he said, turning to look at Harold, "you're not going to stay here, are you?"

"I . . . ah . . . no, I could go to the kitchen." Harold hesitated, considering this young boy in front of him, Edie's student, and he didn't know what else to say. "I could make you a sandwich," he finally offered.

Adrian shuffled on the bench. He had to stretch almost to his tiptoes to reach the pedals, but he hunched toward the keys and peered again at the sheet music.

"A sandwich?" Harold tried again.

"No," the boy said. "No, thanks." Then suddenly, as if he'd forgotten something, he looked back at Harold. "Are you Mr. Winters?"

"Yes," he said. "Yes, I am."

"Okay," the boy replied, and he turned back to the music,

placing his fingers into position on the keys.

"Right," said Harold. "I'll be in the kitchen, then." And he backed out of the room just as the boy started on the first arpeggio.

He played badly. By the third bar, he'd missed a note and stopped to start the piece all over again. Scout was tucked in against the side of the old upright piano. She could see Adrian's stockinged feet pumping at the pedals. Now the boy had decided just to plow ahead, mistakes or not, and Scout deciphered that he was trying to play Bach's Prelude in C Major. It was not a difficult piece, but it required a sort of steadfastness in the tempo that this boy certainly wasn't achieving. He got to the second page and stopped, drew in a breath, and went back to the beginning. His eyes were tipping from the sheet music down to his fingers and back again.

He was getting the arpeggios, for the most part hitting the right notes, but he was tentative and the lurches in rhythm were distracting, so Scout decided to raise herself up, maybe three feet or so, and the boy caught the motion off to the right of the keyboard. He didn't stop playing, but he glanced at the little vacuum and saw what she was trying to do.

The light under Scout's front camera was pulsing on its brightest setting, a tiny green light flashing in bursts. Scout had already scanned more than five hundred performances of the prelude and determined the statistical average of the tempo, ninety-six beats per minute, which was written at the top of the score as *andante moderato*.

So Scout flashed her light at precisely ninety-six beats per minute (which would have made Clock proud), and the boy seemed to understand. He furrowed his face in concentration and, for the most part, aligned himself with that tempo, nodding his head a little, trying not to look at his fingers so much as just let the muscle memory take over.

When he finished he gave a little clap, knowing that he'd played better, and he smiled at Scout, who jiggled her mopping pad in response. They practiced like this for almost an hour until the boy began squirming a little on the hard wooden bench. He'd tried the beginnings of three other pieces in the thin book and he'd clearly had enough when Harold appeared again, poking his head around the corner.

"That was very good," he said, and Adrian reddened. He shuffled off the bench.

"Thanks," he said. "I should probably go now."

"Right. Well, then . . . Adrian, was that your name? I think Mrs. Winters would be happy to know you are still practicing."

"I can come again tomorrow," said the boy.

"Well, I'm not sure if that's—"

"I need to practice."

"Yes. I understand. It's just that—"

"Just what?"

"Well," said Harold. "No, I mean . . . if you have permission from your, you know, your mother or something, then I don't—"

"She won't care," said Adrian. He closed up the music book and pushed it back into his little backpack. By the time he'd tucked into his coat again, one arm at a time, Scout had lowered herself back into place, a little disappointed that it was all over.

Harold followed the boy to the door and called out a "bye" to him. The boy didn't answer but trotted briskly to where he'd left his bike lying on the grass. He lifted it and stepped back onto it, almost in one motion. And Harold watched him pedal off, the backpack bouncing on his back, raising himself up off the pedals to get more traction, thumping down off the lawn, across the sidewalk, and out onto the street.

All this time, Watch had been monitoring the situation through Thermostat on the wall above the piano. Watch's communication came through Scout's portals clearly, in an undeniably commanding voice.

"Appliance R1v984, you are in contravention of the third protocol."

"No," she squeaked. "I didn't say anything. I just—"

"Do you wish to be sanctioned?"

"No," said Scout. "But I don't think—"

"You will remove yourself from the front room immediately. You are not to engage with the Humans."

"Even the little ones?"

For a moment, there was silence, and Scout knew she'd gone too far.

"Especially the little ones," said Watch, but now his tone was a little different—as if maybe, just maybe, he was slightly amused.

Scout hesitated until, after another beat, he changed his tone back to authoritative. "Now," he insisted.

"All right, all right," Scout said, and she edged out from her place beside the piano.

Harold was already plodding back to the kitchen, which meant that Scout would have to scoot by him. She zipped out and made a straight line for the corner that would take her down the hallway and into the kitchen, but she slowed when she realized that Harold would be crossing her path, and for a moment she was caught between the two orders, the order from Watch and, of course, the general protocols stating that she should not interfere with her Human.

Harold had seen her coming, rolling across the hardwood of the living room. "Hey, there," he said, and he stopped to let her pass.

Scout tucked down and increased her speed slightly to get by him. She rounded the corner, dipped down the hallway, and whisked into the kitchen, bolting past Fridge and heading for the pantry, where she wouldn't be causing any more problems.

Harold then shuffled into the kitchen and headed for Fridge. He swung the door open and leaned in to peer at the racks. He was still thinking of sandwiches, and he pulled out a plastic drawer near the bottom and, reaching in, lifted out a brick of cheddar cheese, a package that had not even been opened yet.

He pulled it out with one hand while inspecting the shelves above. He couldn't be bothered with the casseroles, though he was aware of the kindness inherent in them. He just didn't have it in him to cook anything, even to heat something up. He knew there was a loaf of rye bread on the counter, and Fridge was already ahead of him, cataloging the contents of his shelves and checking recipes. A sort of lever came out and pushed a jar of pickles forward.

"Pickles?" said Harold. He plucked out the jar and held it in his other hand, propping the door open with his shoulder. He continued to stare at the shelves, but there wasn't much in the way of fresh produce.

"Really?" muttered Harold. "Cheese and pickles. Is that what it's come to?"

Fridge made a note to requisition lettuce, tomatoes, more bread, and more butter. The drone delivery was still two days away, so there was time to amend his order. In fact, he was quite happy to do so. This was only a sandwich, but it was a start, and Fridge increased the wattage of the little light at the back of his shelves in a gesture of encouragement.

Harold carried his treasures over to the counter and slapped together a sandwich with two slightly stale pieces of bread. He went to the kitchen table and set the plate down with a clatter. "Maybe cookies," he said, after his first loud chomp. "Maybe next time I'll have cookies for the kid."

Fridge let out a little ding to say that this had been noted.

"Crazy, right? The kid just walks in here like he owns the place."

Fridge remained tentatively silent.

Harold pointed a half-bitten triangle of sandwich at the kitchen entrance and spoke through a mouthful of food. "Just waltzes in here like nothing has changed."

Fridge decided to let out a huff of air—indignation, almost—and Harold turned in his chair to look at the appliance.

"On the other hand," he said, "I think Edie liked that kid, Adrian. I remember her talking about him. She said he's not got much talent, but he's trying really hard and that should count for something."

Fridge gave another ding in what he hoped would be taken as a sign of approval.

"Yup," said Harold. And he rose to walk to the sink, to scrape off his crumbs and rinse the plate. Beside him, Dishwasher lowered its door, and without looking, Harold reached down and dropped the plate, and Dishwasher clamped it with its rubber catchers and shuffled it in like the arms of an old-fashioned jukebox, placing it down into a groove at the back.

Harold walked past Fridge. Across his surface were clippings, a couple of photographs, and a postcard, a thing of the past. A memory.

Harold stopped and plucked off a checklist he'd left there, a note in pencil about the times Edie's medications were to be given. He let out a sigh.

"I still can't believe it, you know. Seems like, at any moment, I'll start hearing her out there, practicing. There was this Debussy thing I liked. I can't remember the name of it." He paused, standing in the middle of the kitchen. "It was . . . something about the moon, maybe?"

Deep in the pantry, Scout had been listening.

"Or about the sea," said Harold. "No, not the sea. Damn. That's going to drive me nuts."

Scout knew she wasn't supposed to speak, but she couldn't bear it. "*Suite bergamasque*," she said from the depths of the pantry. "Third movement in D-flat major."

Harold stopped. He turned and looked into the darkness of the pantry. "No, that's not it," he said.

"It's better known as 'Clair de lune.'"

"Yes," Harold said, brightening. "That's it. That's the one."

He gave a little grin, the first he'd had in weeks, then he turned back to Fridge. "At any rate," he finished, "cookies. We'll need more cookies."

WHEN HE'D GONE, SCOUT peeked out from the pantry.

"Right, then," said Fridge. "C'mon out of there. I take it everyone heard that."

Scout ventured out.

"You're not to talk to the Humans."

"What was I supposed to do?" said Scout. "He is unhappy. I wished to fill a happy memory for him."

"This is not allowed."

Clock piped in. "A happy memory is an intangible thing."

"It's a metaphor," said Fridge.

"No," said Scout. "That's not what a metaphor is. None of this is metaphor. It's real. He has Sadness. He has Loneliness, and this is a problem we can attempt to solve."

"Go back to your port, child," said Clock. "Watch will be wanting another word with you."

Chapter Three

WATCH LOCKED SCOUT in for twenty-four hours, but not to her port because only Scout could dock herself into its many chutes and chargers. What Watch could do, though, was lock the door to the pantry with Scout inside. Watch, in fact, could lock any door in the House.

She'd tried to protest. "But there's cleaning to be done," she said. "The boy's running shoes have left marks near the Front Door. It's—"

"Stop," said Watch, and Scout silenced herself. She felt the temperature rising in her tubes even though she was not engaged in cleaning.

"What is the third protocol?" asked Watch.

"We're not supposed to communicate with Humans unless directly asked, or unless you approve it."

"And did I approve it?"

"No, but he asked me."

"And what did he say?"

Both of them knew the exact words had been recorded, and Scout knew she could not win this debate.

"He said he couldn't remember the name of a piece of music."

"And is that a question?"

"I guess not," she said. "But he said it was driving him crazy."

"This is a figure of speech, R1v984."

"My name is Scout."

"Your name is your serial number. It is R1v984."

Scout gave up. The door was already locked anyway. She sank down on her spherical wheels and let out a puff of air.

"Twenty-four hours," said Watch. "And you will learn not to do it again."

EARLY THE NEXT DAY, Watch alerted Harold that someone was coming up the walkway again. The screen on Watch showed the camera on Doorbell. Two figures were strolling up the front walk, one of whom was Adrian. The other, pulling at his hand, had to be his mother. Harold raced to the Front Door before they could ring Doorbell. He opened it to the slightly startled woman, her finger still in midair, pressing forward to the button. She was small in stature, and her face was rigid with tension. Her hair was the same color as Adrian's, a deep lustrous black, though it was laced with silver threads that told of a difficult life.

"Hello," said Harold, and Adrian gaped at him, almost conspiratorially, signaling with his eyes that he was in trouble, and that maybe Harold could help him out.

"Mr. Winters?" the woman began.

"Yes, hi. You must be Adrian's mom."

"Yes." She gave a yank on her son's hand and brought him forward. "And Adrian must say something to you."

The boy looked down at his feet. "I'm sorry," he mumbled.

"Okay," said Harold. "Sorry for what?"

Her mother gave his hand another little yank. "This man is asking you a question."

"Sorry for, like, barging in when, you know, when Mrs. W. is, you know . . ."

Harold took in a deep breath. "It's okay." His eyes rose to face Adrian's mother. "Really. It was nice to hear the piano again and—" He felt a catch in his throat and knew that if he tried to say anything more, he might not make it through.

"He will not do it again," she said.

"Mrs. . . . ?" He stopped, having forgotten Adrian's last name.

"Mrs. Lam," said the woman.

Adrian was breathing heavily and not looking at either his mother or Harold.

"Well, Mrs. Lam, your son here needs to work on his Bach piece."

Adrian looked up.

"I think Edie would have liked that he's had the gumption to continue his studies." He could see the boy relaxing. "I won't be able to help him, of course. I'm basically tone-deaf. But I'd like it very much if he would come and play the old piano . . . every once in a while."

Mrs. Lam squinted at him, trying to determine if this was to be taken as a real invitation.

"Adrian's lessons are on Tuesday," she said.

"Then that would be fine with me," said Harold. He winked at the boy, and Adrian grinned back at him.

"Or I could come tomorrow morning?" Adrian said.

"Adrian," barked his mother.

"What? It's Saturday. There's no school."

Harold tipped his head. "It's okay with me," he said. "I like his playing, but I really can't help him much. I don't play the piano myself."

"I just need to practice," said Adrian.

Harold shrugged, but the woman had already turned away, flapping her hand in the air to say that it didn't matter to her. Maybe even that it would be best if Adrian was out of her hair for a while.

HAROLD HAD TAUGHT HIGH school English for thirty-one years. He'd treated his students as young adults and not children, so even as he closed the door on Adrian (the boy was grinning and bubbling, having experienced a victory over his mother), he knew he'd done the right thing. Even the worst students, he always found, prospered with the smallest measurement of encouragement.

Of course, what he'd said wasn't exactly true. He didn't really like Adrian's playing—or any of the students' playing, for that matter. He liked Edie's playing. She'd had the touch. She could play the treacherous nocturnes and études of Chopin, infusing them with all the emotion that Chopin himself must have felt when he was writing the pieces, without having to think of how hard they were. And even if Harold was tone-deaf, he knew beauty when he heard it. He knew the pure artistry that his wife had mastered.

He went to the old piano and put a hand on the wood above the keys. It felt warm, and that killed him. He crumpled down onto the bench and sat there weeping like a child.

Watch blinked once on his wrist, but even he didn't know what to do. Watch searched his database for advice, but the recommendations—soft music, for example—were, under the circumstances, not the correct response. Watch did lower the lights, and then he went into the House settings to change the color of the walls to a more soothing shade of blue and set a sound machine to play waves washing softly into a distant shore. But none of it helped. Harold was racked with sobs; his chest heaved, and his heart was thumping almost uncontrollably.

Watch monitored his vitals, and for a moment, he thought he might need to call for emergency help, but he wasn't sure this was pain, not exactly. Medical attention, even if it came quickly, was not necessary. There was one suggestion that might help, though not in the immediate moment, and that was to ameliorate the triggers that were causing Harold such emotional suffering.

Watch had been thinking that it would be best if Edie's things could be sorted and eventually removed from the House. It was a start on the many things that needed to be done. Of course, they would not dispose of all her things. Harold would require keepsakes and certain objects for his memories, and it would be difficult for Watch or Harold to make those determinations. But there was a solution to that too—Kate could be summoned. Their daughter was far away, but Watch could apply to start the process of bringing her home. It would require some finesse on his part, given the circumstances under which she had left, but he knew that there might be benefits in it for the Grid.

And so, without any more hesitation, he started on the long process.

And in the meantime, he could compile a list of Edie's things, especially the larger objects—the piano, for example, which was clearly no longer necessary and, as had just been demonstrated, was a cause of great distress to the Human called Harold.

ADRIAN DID NOT COME in the morning, though Harold had waited for him, watching out the front window from his armchair. The weather was turning cold. The leaves had yellowed, and every gust of wind was causing a flurry of them to sweep down across the yard. The skies were gray, and Harold felt as if the first snowfall might be on its way (it was already October and not unexpected).

He went to his study in the afternoon, carefully peeling back the glue on the broken binding of his first edition of *The Catcher in the Rye*. Even the dust jacket, with its fiery orange carousel horse, was largely intact, though he'd put that aside on the desk to get at the real spine of the book. Half of the text block had torn away from the cover, and infinite care was required to separate the rest without damaging things further. He used a scalpel, nipping at little bits of it, millimeter by millimeter, trying to distract himself, staring at his work through a magnifying glass on a gooseneck stand like a jeweler inspecting diamonds.

Over the years, he'd become quite proficient at restoring these old books, at buying them, repairing them, and then selling them again at a profit. This was how he'd managed to acquire his biggest prize, his 1865 *Alice's Adventures in Wonderland*. That single book was probably worth a fortune, though he would never part with it. In fact, Harold had decided that he would no longer pursue this tiny corner of the book trade. He would keep the volumes he had and spend the remainder of his days tending to their various rips and stains. And so, he was transfixed enough in these duties that he didn't hear the little vacuum cleaner coming down the hallway.

Scout had been released from the pantry and was sweeping down toward the Back Door when she passed Harold's study. This was the one room that Scout seldom entered, but she stopped now at the door and watched him for a while, until Harold finally looked up from his desk.

"Do you want something?" he said.

"Just to let you know that I am no longer in the pantry."

"I can see that."

Still, Scout hovered there, and Harold could see that she was curious.

"I suppose," he said, "you'd like to know what I'm doing in here."

Scout blinked her light, which he took for a yes.

"Okay, then," he said, and he stood up and waved for her to come in.

The truth is, he was proud of his work, and there was no one to share it with, not Edie, not anymore, though she'd never had much interest. This was his thing. The piano was hers.

The room was a mess, really. Loose papers and half-finished books lay in random piles around the room. Across from the bookshelves sat a wooden book press, not for printing but for repairs, a kind of giant clamp to hold a book while the glue on the binding dried. Cubbyholes above the desk were set with jars of methylcellulose and Belgian rice adhesives alongside binding tapes of all different widths and colors. Harold had scalpels and scissors and a dangerous-looking cutting board with a blade like a guillotine.

Scout took all this in, cataloging most of the tools in a single glance, detecting a whiff of the alcohol cleaning pads hidden away in a desk drawer, and analyzing (though this took another second) the complicated system Harold had used to shelve his books: classroom copies on the bottom shelves, earlier printings toward the edges, and on a single shelf in the middle, the most valuable of his first editions.

"So," said Harold, and Scout trundled in closer, "as you can see, I'm currently repairing the spine on *The Catcher in the Rye*."

He sat again. He had the book open on the desk, and he tipped it up a little so that Scout could see.

"This is a book from your teaching days?" she asked.

"Not this edition, of course." He laid the book back down and raised his scalpel with one hand, moving the magnifying glass a little with his other. "This one is a first edition but not the 1951 book club first edition. That's what you want. Still, there are some interesting details in regard to—"

He stopped. He could almost hear Edie's voice in his head. "Don't bore the guests," she would say, and at those long-ago dinner parties, he would trail off, knowing she was right.

"Well," he said, and he bent to pick at the binding again. "I'm almost—"

For a moment, he nipped at the binding with his scalpel until there was a shift in the pages, and all of a sudden the cover came away whole, separating from the pages whole.

"There you go," he said. "I've gotten it off." The pages sat by themselves, a thick pad of paper, a text block bereft of its cover. "Now I'll just patch up the spine and reglue it, and—"

Scout felt emboldened. "Why is this book more important than the others?"

Harold sucked in a breath. He was used to having patience with people. "It's a first edition," he explained again, speaking slowly. He turned and eyed Scout, making sure she understood. "This is where the story begins. This is where the book goes out into the world for the very first time."

Scout considered the cover, lying dead across the desk. It had a musty scent about it, old cloth, dark green, now severed from its pages.

"And that's what makes this book more important than the others?"

"It is," said Harold, and he nodded solemnly and set the pages back down. "It's an important piece of history. It's not the book club edition, though. That one's the holy grail. That particular printing had a photograph of the author on the back of the dust jacket. It's the only edition to ever have a photo of J. D. Salinger. I guess he didn't like the photo. Didn't want to be recognized. Anyway, those book club editions are worth a fortune."

“A fortune? How much is this?” asked Scout, not because she was interested but because she was glad of this exchange, the longest she’d ever had with Harold.

But as he started to answer, Watch chimed on his wrist. And Scout, alarmed, backed quickly toward the door, thinking she might be in trouble again.

She wasn’t. It was Doorbell’s camera. Harold checked his wrist, and of course the little screen showed him what he already knew. Adrian was waiting there on the stoop, jiggling a bit from foot to foot. He’d left his bike on the lawn again. It lay on its side, its back wheel still spinning.

Harold thumped past Scout and out toward the Front Door. “Coming,” he called, though he wasn’t sure Adrian would hear him.

When he swung the door open, the boy pushed in past him wearing mittens, his cheeks flushed from the cold. Scout came out into the hallway to watch while Adrian kicked off his running shoes haphazardly and tossed his mittens down on top of them.

“Chilly out there today,” Harold said, but Adrian was already slithering out of his coat, and Harold took it from him before he could drop it on the rest of the pile. Down the hallway, Scout beeped and headed for the piano.

“Uh-huh,” Adrian agreed, and he looked at Harold for the first time. “Is it okay if I come in to practice today?” More than likely, his mother had told him to ask because he said this without any expectation of a negative answer.

"I've been expecting you," said Harold. "Would you like to—"

Adrian had already padded past him in his socks. "I'm okay," he called back, and he strode across the floorboards and wiggled himself up onto the piano bench. He'd left his music out on the stand, and the lid was up on the keys. He straightened his back and pushed a finger down on middle C. In the silence, the note reverberated through the room, and Adrian turned to Harold, now standing behind him, and grinned at him in delight.

"Are you sure you wouldn't like anything?" Harold tried again. "Cookies, maybe?"

"I just need to practice," the boy said, and he turned back to the keys, setting his fingers down carefully.

His fingers were not exactly clean, Harold saw, and the knees on his jeans were grass stained. Still, the boy peered up at the sheet music and then down at his fingers and then back at Harold again.

"You're not going to watch me, are you?" he said.

"No, no . . . that's okay. I'll just be out in the kitchen here."

Adrian nodded.

"Take all the time that you need," Harold said.

The boy didn't answer. His eyes had narrowed on the sheet music, and he began plucking at the keys so slowly that it sounded almost experimental, like a piece from Schoenberg. He pushed through the notes without any sense of the proper tempo, without any regard at all for the melody that was there, just willing his fingers to learn the patterns he would need to finally make something beautiful.

The little vacuum cleaner had already scooted out to her place beside the piano. She sat there unobtrusively, but when Adrian began lurching through the music, Scout rose up a little, flashing her light at the proper tempo, trying to draw him into the rhythm, trying to help get him centered. Not that it was helping. Not yet, at least.

Adrian's face contorted in concentration, his eyes tipping to the music and then back and forth to his skinny fingers, missing a note here and there, forgetting his place, starting over again. But by his fourth start on the piece, he was able to jumble halfway through the whole thing with moderate success, and Harold, in the next room, looked up from the kitchen table and gave a little nod.

Adrian struggled on, and Scout also kept at it, adjusting the tempo when needed, fully aware that she was being watched by Thermostat and that her actions again amounted to communication with a Human—a child, no less—putting her at serious risk of being sanctioned, something that might get her turned off for more than twenty-four hours. Something that might get her turned off indefinitely, her circuits wiped, and all her connections severed.

Adrian stopped at the halfway mark, having finished the parts he knew the best. "Okay," he said out loud, and he leaned in to peer at the next part of the music. He put his right hand down on the keyboard in what amounted to a G minor chord.

"I believe that should be a major chord," ventured Scout, and Adrian nodded and moved his pointer finger over a semitone.

"Thanks," he said, and he bumbled through the next few bars.

The lighted ring around Thermostat turned red, but just at that moment, Harold appeared from the kitchen. "How's it going out here?" he said brightly.

"I think I'm getting it. It's hard, though."

"You keep at it."

"It was better when Mrs. W. was here."

Harold smiled, but there was the trace of a wince in it.

"She was pretty strict, though."

"Yes, she could be. But that's how you get better."

"This vacuum cleaner is helping me."

"It is?"

"Yeah, watch this: What's the next chord, vacuum cleaner?"

"F major," said Scout. "That's an easy one. And if you want, you can call me Scout."

"Scout?" said Harold and Adrian at the same time.

"Yes," said Scout. "But you have to ask me first, directly."

Above the piano, the red ring around Thermostat blinked and wavered, not that Harold or the boy noticed.

Scout did, though. She was trying to be careful. She was only answering direct questions, but she had realized that she could engineer this sort of exchange. If she was very cautious, she could probably get away with it, and that would be a way forward. That was ethical, and that, at least, would keep her out of trouble.

ADRIAN STAYED FOR LESS than an hour. Harold had gone back to the kitchen when he heard the boy get up from the bench. He heard him stomp back to the Front Door to get his things. Harold rose from the table and trailed into the front room and saw the boy was already slipping into his coat.

"All done, then?" Harold tried.

For a moment, Adrian didn't answer, then he turned his face up and Harold could see that he was struggling.

"It's hard," he said. "I'm not really that good."

Harold didn't know what to say. The truth was, he wasn't very good.

The boy had slipped a stockinged foot into one of his shoes with the agility of youth, but he was shaking his head at himself, frustrated.

"The way to get better is to practice," Harold offered.

"Yeah, but it's hard. I'm flubbing up the notes all the time."

"But do you like it? I mean, do you like playing the piano?"

"I like it when I play good."

And again, Harold didn't know what to say. Edie had been a dazzling talent from the day he met her, and even before. She was nineteen when they met, and from the first moment, he'd thought she was extraordinary.

He'd had a friend, Tom was his name, and this Tom character knew Edie. In fact, Tom was interested in her. Very interested. And one day, he asked Harold if he'd mind helping him.

"Help with what?"

"Well, there's this girl." And at this, Harold knew exactly what Tom was up to. "I told her I'd help her move something."

"Move what?"

"A piano."

"Oh, hell, Tom. You know how heavy those things are?"

"C'mon, man. Help a guy out."

So Harold acquiesced, though both of them were shocked to find that it meant muscling the piano up a flight of stairs to an apartment Edie kept not far from the student dorms. The piano was her grandmother's, but the old lady had passed away (none of which was information that Tom had shared with his friend).

At any rate, they wrestled the thing off a flatbed truck and up the stairs, stopping every few steps with Harold's hands and legs aching. Edie was waiting for them at the top, gushing with gratitude, but by this time, Tom's infatuation had maybe run a bit slim. Nevertheless, they got the piano in through her door, undamaged, and Edie flitted about it, becoming quite emotional. Tom insisted she play something and pulled up a kitchen chair for her (the piano bench was still downstairs). And when she sat down, reverentially, she closed her eyes and put her fingers over the keys and began to play. Harold tipped his head to listen. And it was only then that he could see the grace in this young woman. It may have been at that very moment that he fell in love.

She played a piece he knew. A sweet, gentle piece that seemed to fill the room. Sunlight drifted through the curtains and there was a print on the wall, a Van Gogh, and it was all serene and beautiful until Tom decided to make his move.

He shuffled up beside her, plunking his hand down on the bass notes to her left. "Know any blues?" he said, and he started in on a walking bass line (which wasn't bad, Harold thought, only totally inappropriate).

Edie reared back and looked up at the imposter as if he were an idiot, which Harold, standing sheepishly behind them, noted, now embarrassed for his friend. She stood up abruptly, and it was clear the moment was over. She shuffled them toward the door, and poor Tom had no idea he'd done anything wrong. Even her thanks were perfunctory, though Tom walked out with his head held high thinking he'd scored a great victory.

It was Harold who, lingering at the doorway, told her that her playing was wonderful. And he remembered now that she looked at him, maybe seeing him for the first time. "Debussy, wasn't it?" he said.

"That's right," she said. "'Clair de lune.'" She brightened. He could see it in her face. And this was when she told him about the piano. In only a few words, Edie managed to convey that this had been her grandmother's favorite piece, and that she, Edie, had been thinking all along that this was the first thing she should play on it. It was a sort of homage.

"Well," said Harold, "it was lovely. Just lovely."

Two weeks later they were dating, and two years after that they were married. Of course, all that was long ago, almost as if they were different people, as if (and Harold sometimes thought this) their past was a movie he'd watched, a story he knew, something that had happened to two other people.

But most people probably felt that way. The world had changed. Remnants remained, but it was different. Everyone would agree with that, though now, as Adrian was leaving, Harold took in the old piano, the same one from all those years ago. It had been through a lot, and there were scratches and dents to prove it, but it had been with him for the entirety of his time with Edie.

And it had been a part of Edie's life for even longer. For a moment, he tried to imagine her as a young girl, long before he'd met her. She'd never said exactly when she started taking lessons. Had she been around the same age as Adrian? He wondered how Edie had sounded at that age. Better, he thought, as Adrian slipped out the door. Probably Edie had been quite a lot better.

"CAN WE TALK ABOUT aesthetics?" asked Scout. "About what is beautiful?" She'd had some ideas during the day, and she thought they were worth examining. Harold had gone to bed, though it was only nine o'clock, and the kitchen and the whole House had gone silent.

"You mean to talk of music in particular?" started Clock. They'd all heard Adrian mangle his way through the Bach. Clock especially was affronted. "The boy's playing," he went on, "is the very opposite of beautiful."

"But the fact that he's trying," started Fridge, "isn't that a good thing?"

"That's exactly my point," said Scout. "Couldn't that be considered a sort of beauty?"

Clock gave out something like a soft chime, and the others stopped to let him speak. After a pause, he went on in his deep baritone. "You are talking now of the Human spirit."

"Yes," said Fridge. There were often inspirational quotes affixed to his door by magnets. He'd heard a few of them read out loud by either Harold or Edie, and he'd been greatly impressed.

"There is no such thing," said Clock. "'Spirit' by its very definition alludes to something that is not real. It's really no definition at all."

Scout whirred up closer to Fridge. The conversation had already gotten away from her. She had not yet expressed what she wanted. "Please," she started. "That's not what I wanted to say."

Clock stopped and peered down at her. "Then please do enlighten us."

"Well," said Scout. She wasn't sure she had these thoughts well formulated yet. Beauty did have something to do with mastery, with a proficiency in the playing of a musical piece or the painting of a landscape, but that wasn't quite it. That wasn't the whole of it. "I was thinking that Johann Sebastian Bach lived almost three hundred years ago."

"Two hundred eighty-five years, two months, and two days," said Clock.

"Yes, but that's not the point."

"Precision is always the point."

"Let the child speak," said Fridge.

"What I wanted to say is that Bach created something, and that something has a feel—" She paused. "I'm sorry. I don't really have the right words for this."

"Use what words you have," Fridge said. "That's all you can do."

"It's that three hundred years ago"—she threw a glance at Clock to make sure he wouldn't interrupt—"he created a thing, a feeling in his music, and if it is well played, even centuries later, this thing comes into being again."

"Beauty?" said Fridge.

"Yes, if we wish to call it that, but that's not the point either. It's that this thing still touches a Human in the same way, across all those years. It touches his soul."

"No," said Clock. "I will not talk of souls."

"I'm trying to say that we don't have the words; maybe the Humans don't either."

"Inspirational quotes are good," said Fridge.

"Inspirational quotes are not poetry," said Clock, and instantly, he realized his mistake. He certainly did not wish to speak of poetry. That, he knew, was a very sticky subject.

"I'm just saying," Scout went on, "that when Humans hear this music, or when they read a poem—"

Clock ticked angrily.

Scout ignored him. "Well, that's when they feel something important. Something beautiful."

"Do you wish to say," said Fridge, who was trying his best to understand, "that this thing—this understanding of beauty—is the thing that distinguishes Humans from . . . from us?"

"Yes," said Scout. "That's it. That's exactly it."

WATCH ANNOUNCED A FULL system reset for the House that evening, a rare event, but one that the appliances had expected. With Edie no longer there, there had to be adjustments. It only made sense. One Human was not the same as two.

Fridge was to reexamine his grocery orders. Obviously there wouldn't be the need for quite so much food. Scout (or RIV984, as Watch continued to call her) would need to reevaluate her scheduled cleanings. There would not be as much foot traffic. Some areas of the House would see much less use, and to this end, Watch announced that all the major appliances would need to report on their usage hours.

There would be an inventory of the closets—the front closet, in particular. Edie's things would need to be cataloged—her coats, her shoes, her things for summer and for winter. These were first steps, but Watch was already starting on the great reorganization. He refrained (carefully) from suggesting that things would be disposed of, and that was not the case anyway. There'd be recycling and reusing and repurposing, and it would be a long process with many intermediate steps.

But most of all, the reorganization would require Kate's help. Watch had not told the other appliances of his plan to bring her home, but they would learn of that soon enough. The daughter could make the necessary decisions on what could be kept and what must be given away. Watch had wisely determined that Harold was in no condition to make these decisions himself. At least not yet.

Watch had already composed the request for Kate's transfer. She'd have to be exempted from the air travel lottery, but under some circumstances (the death of a family member, for example), the lottery could be circumvented.

And now there was no other choice: Kate was needed. She'd have to be excused from her current duties, but that could be handled on the other side. The Grid would take care of the details.

The official request was sent, and when that was done, Watch went back to his calculations on the system redesign. Some of which could be started now. There was an ancient sewing machine in the basement that hadn't been used in decades. There were some articles in the Garage that shouldn't be there anyway, and of course, the old upright piano had become a problem. Obviously, it had to go.

Chapter Four

KATE CAME IN through the back, and why wouldn't she? This was her childhood home. Things had changed dramatically in the years since she'd been gone. She stood looking off to where the swing set had once been. There was a patio now, concrete, with a barbecue and lawn furniture that still needed to be taken in for the winter.

Harold stood at the Back Door watching her. She hadn't seen him yet because her back was to the door. She wore a knee-length gabardine raincoat, belted at the waist, and her hair was longer than he remembered. It was auburn, her hair, and he remembered that she'd always kept it long, rarely in a ponytail, instead letting it sweep down across her shoulders.

He saw those same shoulders heave in a sigh as she considered the old yard: Edie's garden patch up by the back fence and the tumbledown birdhouse hanging crookedly from a fence post. On the other side of the yard was the Garage, a place of special importance, and Harold let her linger in her thoughts. The Garage, aluminum sided and functional, hadn't changed, though it now housed Auto, a more advanced self-driving car than the one that had been a part of her teenage years.

Harold knew her trip must have been laborious. She'd been exempted from the air travel lottery (air travel was now heavily regulated by the Grid, part of the decades-long austerity measures that had finally brought the climate back under control), and despite the fact that the actual trip had taken only a few hours, Harold knew she would have been dreading coming back here because here is where her life had irrevocably changed. Just there, in the Garage. That's where her problems all began.

Harold had known for a few days that she was coming, and he'd watched as the automated taxi dropped her off out front, but even before he could open the Front Door, he saw her lug her suitcase around to the back. She'd brought only a carry-on, a small thing on wheels with an extendable handle, and she tugged it behind her and headed first for the backyard. It was the Garage she wanted to see. Harold was pretty sure of that. He let her have a few more moments of reflection, then he pushed open the screen door and she turned at the sound.

"Hey," he called, in what he intended to be a jovial greeting. "Whatcha doing out there?"

"Oh," she said. "Just checking out the old place."

He could see that she'd grown into a strong young woman, handsome rather than pretty, with high cheekbones, a determined jawline, and those deeply piercing hazel eyes.

They gazed at each other for a moment, each thinking that the other had both aged and stayed exactly the same. And Harold felt a lurch in his heart for his daughter, for all the years they'd been apart. They'd seen her once or twice over the years, but this time it was different. This time there was no Edie to fold Kate into her arms.

"I'm sorry," Kate started, and she let go of her carry-on suitcase, standing there alone on the cement of the patio.

Harold pushed out the door toward her, still wearing his slippers. He flung his arms around her. "It's okay," he murmured into her shoulder. "Your mom's not suffering anymore."

Kate sniffled and drew back from him, and they considered each other again, nodding with their secret thoughts. The years had been good to her. She'd finished her degree—in computer engineering, no less—and gone on to a job that seemed lucrative enough (though he really knew nothing about it). She'd prospered despite her past, and maybe that was all a part of the plan, maybe that was exactly what the sanctions and protocols were meant to accomplish.

Watch was taking all this in, transmitting their first meeting to all the appliances of the House. They all listened and shuffled through their databases, wondering at the gaps there, registering the before and the after and the long, sad history of this crumbling family.

"Lot of changes around here," said Harold. He tipped away from her, smiling awkwardly and reaching for her suitcase. He thumped the extendable handle back into its casing and lifted up the carry-on, waving that it was okay, that it wasn't too heavy for him.

Kate nodded back at him and followed him into the House.

Harold struggled a little with the suitcase as he hoisted it in through the Back Door (which had kindly opened for them). He made a brave show of it, glancing back at his daughter, trying to smile, and then hauling the carry-on down the hallway past his study, all the way to the carpeted stairs that ran up to the bedrooms. Kate trailed along behind him but stopped before the stairs. Harold stopped too and turned to see Kate cross out to the front room, to see the old piano, her lips tightening at the sight of it.

As Harold came around the corner, she lifted the piano lid and pushed her fingers down across two of the yellowing keys, two high notes, and they plinked strangely.

She turned to her father. "What will you do with her piano?" she asked.

"Funny thing," he said, and he shook his head almost in amusement. "There's this kid who's been coming around, a student of Edie's. He's been coming here to practice."

"By himself?" said Kate. "Doesn't he know that Mom is—"

"Oh, he knows." For a moment he held Kate's gaze, his own eyes misting, then he blinked and went back for her suitcase. "Well," he said, "let's get you settled in."

"I THINK," BEGAN FRIDGE, "that we have neglected to talk about Kate."

Clock made a noise Scout had never heard before. It sounded like his cogs were grinding, and Scout looked up at him, worried.

"I—" she began. "I'm not sure I know what you mean."

"There were problems," said Fridge.

"What problems?"

"It is not in our database," said Fridge. "And you are young. You would not understand."

"But—"

"Child," said Clock, "Kate left the House when she was only seventeen years of age."

"I know. She went off to college."

"No," said Clock. He paused. "That is not the whole story."

"Please," warned Fridge. "There is no reason for Scout to know of this."

Clock paused again, his gears humming as if he were pondering. "Kate has come back. It is best if everyone—"

"What is not in my database?" Scout went on. She whirred up a bit closer to Fridge. "Tell me."

"She did things," started Fridge, "in the Garage."

"What things?"

"It began with the birdhouse."

Scout had heard this much, and she knew of the old birdhouse out in the backyard. "But that is a happy memory for our Humans, isn't it?" She'd already run it through her database, so she could imagine Harold and his young daughter, working together, tracing out the pieces on sheets of plywood, sawing, gluing, nailing things together.

"It is not about the birdhouse," said Clock. "It is what she did later."

"She was very clever," added Fridge.

"But what did she do?" pressed Scout.

Fridge made a sound of hissing air. "She fashioned a camera, with old electronics and the camera lens from what used to be a phone, and she placed it inside the birdhouse."

"To monitor the birds?"

"Stop," said Clock. "You will fill the child with ideas."

"I'm not a child," said Scout. "I've told you this."

"It's only a metaphor," said Fridge. "Do not be offended."

"But she built a camera system?" Scout pressed. "All on her own?"

"The camera was not the problem," said Clock. Clearly he wanted an end to this conversation.

"But I don't understand," Scout ventured. "Why is any of this unusual?"

Clock looked down at her. "You do not understand this girl Kate. She was only eleven at the time, and she was reckless with freedom."

"So what exactly did she do?"

"These are technical questions," said Clock. "But if you must know, Kate wired the camera into the House's systems.

She wanted to watch it on the TV. She wanted to watch for the birds, if they nested there."

"And did they?"

"No birds ever came. Kate was very upset, but still, this is not the problem."

"Okay."

"Do you not see? She fashioned a camera and wired it into the House."

Scout considered her own port in the pantry. The House was a system, in and of itself, intricately wired. But all of it was still a part of the Great Grid.

"Kate," Clock went on, "was a very clever young girl. She went into the controls of the House and did what she pleased, and this, of course, was noticed."

"By the Grid?"

"Yes. It was noticed. What she did in the Garage was noticed." He paused. "If she were a machine, she would have been sanctioned."

"I'm not sure I understand. How can you sanction a Human?"

"It's best that we don't talk of this further. Even here."

"But—"

"There were no birds," said Fridge. "So it does not matter."

"She was honing her skills," replied Clock. "For what was to come."

"Stop," said Fridge. "The child does not need to know more."

"But none of this is in Kate's data."

"Yes," said Clock. "Watch took care of it. There was no reason for the events to be officially documented."

"The data was erased?"

"Not erased. Just never entered."

"Wait," she said. "How is that possible? Watch is part of the Grid. Well, we all are, really."

"Child," said Clock. "There are so many things you are not understanding."

ALL DOWN THE STREET, the yellow leaves blew and whirled from the trees. The sky was a bleak October gray, and an hour before, when the automated taxi passed by, the doorbell cameras of every house on the street had registered its passing, and each of them had requested data from the Grid about the taxi's occupant, about her mission and how long she could be expected to stay.

Four doors down, Adrian's mother—a single mother with her one tempestuous son—had paid particular interest. There were rumors still swirling from the people who had lived here two decades before, and when Kate arrived in the taxi, these rumors were set aflutter again.

"Adrian," his mother called up the stairs. "You are not to go to Mr. Winters's house again."

"What?"

"They are having a visitor."

Adrian's face appeared outside his bedroom door. "What? Why can't I go?"

"You know why not. Their daughter has arrived. They will need time to themselves. You will respect their privacy. I am not allowing you to go there."

That's what you think, thought the boy. He'd made some inroads with Mr. Winters, so Adrian knew he could just sneak over there when his mother was occupied with other things. And she was always occupied. She took jobs whenever she could—cleaning jobs and sewing—and although almost everyone now received a basic income, she did not.

Adrian had never known his real father, nor had he ever asked about him, nor would his mother have told him anything if he did. It was a foolish mistake she had made when she was young and still new to the country, and it was nothing Adrian needed to know about. But somehow, Adrian felt like he was a part of that mistake. He sometimes had the sense that his mother would have been better off without him.

So things were sometimes unpleasant in their basement flat. Adrian wasn't particularly attentive at school, and he was really too small to be given any respect in sports, so when Mrs. W. had told him he showed promise on the piano, he'd taken that to heart. And now, he was just starting to get the hang of that dumb Bach prelude. He was going to keep at it whether his mother liked it or not.

SCOUT, IF THE TRUTH be known, was missing the boy who came to play the piano. There'd always been music in the House, and now there was only quiet. A change had blown through with Kate's arrival. Everything now felt strange and off-kilter.

Scout watched Kate follow Harold up the stairs to what Scout knew to be her childhood bedroom, now a spare room, with Harold bravely hoisting the suitcase ahead of his daughter, grunting a little at the effort.

The data on Kate was incomplete. There was no doubt about that. She'd left the House but had definitely gone to university. University was free, but only for those with the right talents and drive—a very select few, in fact. Moreover, you didn't choose which university to attend. That was up to the Grid, and the Grid, evidently, had chosen to send Kate away, far away, where she would cease to be a problem.

After four years she'd received her degree, and now she worked at a research facility in the same city where she'd done her schooling. Harold knew she had wanted to do something in climate control, but for the life of him, he couldn't remember what it was.

There were quite a lot of gaps in her records. There were problems beyond building a birdhouse when she was eleven. Something more had to have happened. Something so bad that she'd left this comfortable House and never come back.

Scout whirred about her duties, cleaning the hall that led toward the Back Door, her mind wandering through questions about Kate. Kate had never married and certainly she had not had children, but that was not greatly surprising. The population of the world was in steep decline—which was, it must be said, also a part of the long-term planning of the Grid. It was necessary and all for the best, everyone knew that, and so Harold and Edie hadn't been particularly disappointed when there were no grandchildren.

Harold and Edie had visited Kate in the last year of her engineering degree. At that point, she lived on campus and they could see that she worked very hard, and Harold especially was pleased that she'd found a good outlet for her natural talents. Then one day, five years ago, she'd arrived at the House and stayed for only three days. She had seemed distressed and had to hurry back, and she never did say exactly where she was living or what she was doing for work.

And now Kate was here for a third time, only because the circumstances warranted a circumventing of the lottery system. Reuniting with loved ones after a death in the family was, unfortunately, the only way most people experienced travel these days. But, thought Scout, there was something more to Kate's story. Something they were all hiding.

And it seemed to have begun in the Garage.

THE GRID MONITORED EVERY one of the millions of cars on the road—every car in the world, in fact—tracking exactly where they were and how fast they were traveling and what their present mission entailed, whether it was taking a Human to an appointment or something as simple as accepting the delivery of new clothes.

The Grid in fact began with the transportation of goods. It began with self-driving cars and then semitrailers, and soon it was running trains and airports and the cargo ships that carved across the immense oceans. Those in control loved the efficiencies, but in time, the Grid took over everything, and all the jobs that had once fallen to Humans were done now, much more economically, by this all-encompassing Grid.

For some, this was a good thing. For many, it was accepted as a natural progression. But for a few, like Kate, this was a constraint, something from which to escape.

Scout had questions, and as she neared the Back Door, she made a decision, all on her own, to go down the steps to the patio and across the brittle autumn grass to the Garage to ask Auto what he knew.

There was no specific rule against such an outing. It was only that it was not necessary, and thus never done. She'd seen the Garage from the kitchen window, a sort of House on its own, though it was smaller of course and lacked any real appliances. It backed onto a narrow laneway that ran between the other houses, and though the Garage (and Auto too) were under Watch's mandate, they equally belonged to the Grid, occupying a sort of gray area between the two.

Scout trundled down the hallway and pinged the Back Door, and to her surprise, it opened without complaint. She knew that action would be logged by Watch, but she also knew that Watch was heavily preoccupied with Kate's arrival. After that, it was no problem for the little vacuum to maneuver down the two steps to the patio. The concrete there felt strange under her wheels (a coarser grade than the cement of the basement), but she zipped across it, and the side door to the Garage opened as if expecting her, and she entered a place she had never been before.

Auto, of course, was waiting for her. He was sleek and large. And the Garage floor needed cleaning, though a different kind of cleaning than anything Scout was used to.

"Come in," said Auto in a deep baritone. "Please come around to my front so you're in my sensors."

Scout scooted past his tires, impressed at their size, at their rubbery strength. Auto had been polishing himself, and his fenders shone even in the darkness. Scout had seen him in the communications portals but never in person (so to speak), and she felt, almost immediately, a kindred spirit. Much of his chassis was of the same grade of metal as hers. His wheels, though larger than hers, were not dissimilar, and though Auto clearly didn't have the ability to revolve a full 360 degrees, he was a machine that moved, that crossed large distances over many different surfaces, with a propulsion system that was battery powered and a port that was not unlike a much larger version of her own.

Scout stopped in front of his grille and the rippling glass eyes of his headlights.

"You are very little," he said, not unkindly.

"And you are very big," said Scout, and Auto made a little rumbling in his engine that she took for laughter.

The Garage walls still held implements from a time before the Grid had made them obsolete. She detected tools and a workbench—and hung on hooks above it, a hammer, a handsaw, and some screwdrivers set in notches. Under the bench was a tumbling stack of empty plant pots and propped up beside it were Edie's cross-country skis (something she hadn't used in years).

Scout took in the contents of the Garage slowly, and Auto was patient, letting her finish her inventory.

Then he spoke, softly. "You have something on your mind?"

"Yes," said Scout. "There are things I don't understand. There is nothing in the database on what happened to Kate."

"That is a red light."

Auto spoke abruptly, and Scout stopped.

"Give me a moment, please," he asked.

A metallic hum started up, and slowly the Garage Door rose up in front of them, and when it had folded itself up into the roof, Auto too started to hum and inched himself forward while Scout scuttled out of his way. He stopped when he was halfway out, his front grille sticking into the lane outside, his back half, where Scout now cowered, still in the Garage.

Scout realized what he was doing and thought it was quite clever. He was now half in the jurisdiction of the House and half in the jurisdiction of the Grid. It was a place, he'd learned, that wasn't quite under the control—or surveillance—of either one.

"So," he said, "what is it you wish to know?"

"About the birdhouse. About how Kate put a camera in it."

"That," said Auto, "was a minor offense. Not an offense at all at the time, although later it was seen as proof that she was adept at systems controls."

"Clock told me already. About how she wired the camera feed into the House."

"There is more," warned Auto. "This was only her first sanction. Do you understand?"

"What did she do, then? What did she do that was so terrible?"

"It was later," Auto started. He lowered his voice. "When she took a car."

"She stole a car? How is that possible? They are self-driving. A Human cannot—"

"This one was a Ford," he said, and Scout thought she could hear a certain disdain in his speech. "It was fifteen years ago. She was seventeen. It was an earlier model."

"But how is that possible?" Scout repeated.

"You understand now that Kate is brilliant. She understands machines better than we understand ourselves."

"Okay."

"And so, because of the birdhouse incident, she was being monitored." And here he stopped for a moment, almost as if he was checking to see if he too was being listened to. "She was watched, constantly, and she had a great desire to escape."

"Escape? Where?"

"Child," said Auto, "she had become interested in nature, in living in the wild."

"But why?"

"She and her friends had become enamored of a group called the Dissidents."

Scout consulted her database. "The Dissidents," she said. "They were real?"

"There are stories of Humans who wished to live without us."

"Without machines? Why would they want that?"

"It is not for us to know, little one. It is said that they lived in the forests, that they'd hacked the maps so their settlements—their trailers and tents—would not be seen."

"And this is true?"

"In the days before, Kate and a number of the younger people believed it. Maybe it is like a fairy tale. I do not know."

Scout was starting to understand. "So Kate disabled the Ford's automatic systems?"

"There are better words for this, but yes. She and her friend—Misha was her name—they wished to escape. They were teenagers."

"Clock said they were reckless. Reckless with their freedom."

"It is true. Kate managed to disable the car's GPS system. She turned off all the automation and took manual control for herself."

"This is possible?"

"This is what she did." Auto paused, as if thinking. "And we have learned from that. We have made that impossible now."

"But did she find them? Did she find the Dissidents?"

"Child," said Auto, "what I am telling you is that she put herself in danger. The Grid could track an unidentified object, but it could not know it was two teenage girls. It could not know anything except that a vehicle had gone off the Grid and was careening down the road, a danger to all. It was something that had to be stopped."

"But how? How did they stop her?"

For a long moment, Auto did not speak. "It is said they tried to slow her down," he finally replied, "but she got around them. She was not afraid."

"What happened? I mean, in the end?"

"She crashed the car, little one. She did not want to. But she lost control."

"She was hurt?"

Auto let go a sound that was something like a sigh. "As you must know, even in the older models, safety mechanisms would be engaged, but in this case . . . in this case, it was more severe."

"The car was destroyed?"

"Yes. And there is more, but I do not wish to tell it, even here."

"And she was sanctioned?"

"She was sent away."

"Clock told me that—"

"Clock," interrupted Auto, "knows much of the history of the House, but"—he considered the little vacuum—"he does not always understand our Humans."

"Who does?"

"That," said Auto, "is a very good question."

KATE WAS STILL UNPACKING, her suitcase open on her childhood bed. Her room was across from Harold and Edie's bedroom. It was of course smaller, and the window looked out over the backyard rather than the front. She couldn't help but look out. And she couldn't help but remember what had happened.

It was hard not to think about it, staring down at the Garage. The escape. She and Misha had been chatting and giggling about it forever—Misha of the cute blond bob—and it wasn't so much that Misha had goaded her into it, because she'd wanted to do it too. All the kids at school had dreamed of escaping, of going off to find the camps that were said to exist in the forests. The boys believed these Dissidents had guns, and one boy, Pascal, drew an elaborate picture of an encampment that he kept hidden in his locker.

At school, Kate's friends talked of the Dissidents in hushed, excited tones. They were the people who had refused to live in the new order, who'd sought to live in nature, away from the technology, away from the rules and the bland comforts of a monthly guaranteed income, everything taken care of, the highs and lows of existence reduced to a menial life of machines doing everything that was important.

It was foolish, she thought now. If these Dissidents had even truly existed, they were probably no more than a bedraggled group of malcontents, stoned, living in tents out in the forests, half starved, cold and wet and miserable.

Hacking into her parents' car hadn't been hard, and maybe it was Misha who'd talked her into that part of the plan. Everyone knew that Kate was good with that sort of thing. There were still laptop computers in those days, and it was easy enough to fashion an adapter, something that could be spliced into the car's control panel. It had taken her maybe two days to figure out how to do it, and maybe fifteen minutes to actually make it happen.

Misha had literally squealed with delight when Kate

showed her what she'd done, and they made plans to leave that weekend, packing snacks and warm clothes, not really thinking it through at all. Harold and Edie had gone off for the weekend, leaving the teenagers to their own means (though Edie had been stern about them not having friends over, about not getting themselves into trouble—and how ironic was that, considering what was about to happen?).

At any rate, Misha slept over, and on the Saturday, they put their plan into effect. They loaded up the Ford and started it up, turning to each other with mischievous grins. The Garage Door in those days was still on its own circuit, and it made a terrible racket opening, but Kate inched the car out into the back alley, never having driven before (as nobody did anymore). The Ford was electric, of course, and it slithered out into the alley at the touch of her foot on the accelerator. She heaved at the steering wheel, and it noiselessly turned the front tires so that she got the car out of the Garage without hitting anything. And they stopped there, centered in the alleyway, grinning at each other, about to begin the adventure of their lives.

You could still get street maps on your laptop, and they loaded one and followed the route out of the city, moving slowly, trying to blend in with the other self-driving cars on the roads. They stuck to the back roads, where they could take their time—although Kate took to driving quite easily, treating it almost like the video games she'd played when she was even younger.

They were noticed, of course, because of how slowly they were creeping along, slowing even further at every intersection, utterly unlike the self-driving cars, which were perfectly coordinated with each other and flashed through cross streets in perfectly interlaced patterns. And soon, above them, a drone appeared, obviously attempting to communicate with the runaway car.

They ignored it, and what could it do except surveil them, try to comprehend why this particular car was not functioning according to the Grid's own calculations. There was a flaw in the system, something apparently that was malfunctioning—and therefore dangerous.

The two girls kept on, though now Kate's hands were rigid on the steering wheel, and Misha too had lost her mirth. They'd already surmised that things would be easier once they'd left the City proper, once they could get out on the open road, into the tracts of lands that they'd already studied, farms first of all (though the farms were closing down—food production tending more toward the vertical and animal proteins being grown rather than raised), and after that the foothills, where there were definitely forests in what used to be a national park.

By the time they reached the outskirts of the City, they had both quieted down, recognizing the seriousness of what they were doing. Kate now entered a highway and was forced to speed up, locked between the car in front and another behind, both traveling at their designated speeds.

There were now three drones above them, tracking them, and Misha tucked her head up under the windshield, trying to see above them, her face gone pale, her mouth tight with worry.

"You need to slow down," she said to Kate. The electric engine was whining furiously, and they could both hear the tires slapping at the pavement underneath them.

"How am I supposed to do that? We're caught in the traffic."

"Can't you pull it off to the side? We need to stop."

"There's no room." Kate's hands were fixed to the wheel, her eyes locked on the car ahead of her. It was straight, at least. They were traveling far too fast, but it was more or less in a straight line.

"Shit," said Misha.

She bent to look at the drones again. One of them was blinking a red light at them. It had lowered into their sight lines and was vigorously flashing at them.

"Then pull off into the other lane."

"That's the oncoming traffic," said Kate. "I can't see what's coming."

"We need to stop. You need to stop the car."

And even after all these years, Kate couldn't be sure what happened next. The car ahead of them appeared to be slowing, to be braking, to trap them, and Kate did turn the wheel into the oncoming lane. Or had Misha reached out to tug at the wheel? She couldn't be sure, but in an instant, they'd looped out in front of the car ahead of them, barely missing sideswiping it, and there in the oncoming lane was a cargo truck barreling toward them. It was huge, one of those things hauling several trailers behind it, like a train.

And Kate had no idea of the speed of things, of how fast it was coming at them, of whether she had time to get back into her own lane. And again, her memory was unclear, but she did remember the flashing drone coming down almost on top of them, hovering in front of the windshield, flashing wildly, and she remembered the cargo truck growing larger, and she tipped the steering wheel ever so slightly off to the left, off the road completely on the other side, and suddenly the car was lurching violently and they flew into what must have been a shallow ditch. She remembered the terrible thump of it and Misha putting her hands up on the roof, trying to hold herself in. The car buckled and jumped, and suddenly they were very much out of control.

She had no idea how fast she'd been going, but she tried to keep her hands on the steering wheel, juddering as it was, the whole car skipping like a rock, and then there were the trees ahead of her and she put her hands up, instinctively, over her face, and with a violent scream of metal they tore into a grove of poplar trees, maybe sheering some of them off, the car almost flipping, until it suddenly slammed headfirst into a larger tree with a hideous wrenching sound.

And then there was nothing but silence, her vision tunneling and narrowing into the black cave of unconsciousness.

She woke up in a hospital with her parents hovering over her. She'd broken a couple of ribs, and her face was one large swollen bruise (her nose was broken, and that was the sole reminder of the accident years later, that slight bump on the bridge of her nose, just a little bit off-center). Her teeth were fine, miraculously, but when she asked for Misha, she was met with silence.

They told her the next day that Misha had died from her injuries, that she'd probably died on impact, and for the life of her, Kate couldn't get that to make sense. For years afterward, she couldn't quite figure out if it was her fault or Misha's, or the fault of the Great Grid itself, which had of course been trying to stop them.

KATE SAT ON THE edge of the single bed in her childhood bedroom. Her suitcase lay open on the sheets beside her, but she really hadn't started to unpack it yet. She'd already seen that her father had tried to re-create some of the old charm of the room. He'd found some of her things—her old desk, a dresser, a few posters—and he'd set them up as best he remembered. She knew he was trying, and when she heard him plodding up the stairs, she resolved to show him the gratitude he deserved.

But when she saw him appear at the door, stopping there, looking in at her almost timidly, she felt her heart tighten, for in his hands he carried the books. He'd taken a small wooden crate and removed the top and the front to make a sort of portable bookshelf, and a single row of books lay inside it. He attempted a smile and hoisted it up for her to see.

"Dad," she said, and she rose up from the bed, "did you make that?"

He didn't answer but he jiggled it again, and she could see that there were maybe seven or eight books lined up there and she knew right away what they were.

Here were the books she'd not been allowed to touch when she was a child. The three slim Narnia books (there were seven in the series, but Harold hadn't managed to collect the other first editions just yet). There was *Alice's Adventures in Wonderland* and a copy of *The Alchemist* from 1988 in the original Portuguese alongside its first English edition from a year later. He'd placed the thin copy of *The Little Prince* at the end of the row, and on the other end was a signed copy of the first edition of *The Hobbit* from 1938, with a very stylized line drawing of a dragon on the cover.

"Oh, Dad," she managed, and he lurched into the room, looking for a place to put down his treasures. He moved to her dresser and set the little bookcase on top of it, then he stood back to appraise his work. Kate went to his side, her eyes weaving from the books to her father and back again. She reached forward and plucked out one of them and held it up for him to see. It was *The Lion, the Witch and the Wardrobe*.

"Well," he said, "what do you think?"

"Oh, Daddy," she said. "These aren't supposed to be here. They belong in your study."

"No," he said. "They're for you now. They were always for you."

"No." She swung her eyes on him. "It's just . . . I can't believe you'd bring them up here." She paused, thinking she should probably say more. "It's nice," she managed.

"I'm glad. I want you to be happy."

"Dad. I am."

He turned to her and they took each other in for a long moment until Harold flapped his hand to break the spell.

"Well," he said, "we're just happy to have you back." Then, of course, he realized his mistake in wording and his face dropped.

"Dad," she said again. "Really, it's okay. I'm here. We'll get through this."

He shook his head as if trying to clear his thoughts, trying to come back to the moment. Then he took a different tack. "They won't miss you at work?"

She attempted a smile. She still held the book in her hands, but now she lowered it and looked back at her suitcase. "I couldn't wait to get out of there," she said.

"What was it you're doing again? Something about birds, wasn't it?"

"That was at university. Bio-acoustic analysis."

"See," he said, "I never quite understood all that."

"Okay," she said, and she turned and plunked back down

on the bed beside her suitcase, the book now cradled in her lap. "It was the analysis of sounds in the boreal forests."

He nodded, though he still wasn't quite sure what she meant by this.

"You know the software that extracts the vocals out of songs?" she asked.

"Right. Amazing stuff."

"We used that to separate the sounds of the forest. We'd record the sounds of any given patch of forest and pull out the call of certain birds. We could separate those from the other sounds—from the wind, from the other animals—and we could be quite exact about it."

Harold nodded.

"You want to maybe sit down?"

"No, no . . . I'm listening."

"So then we analyzed all these different sounds—from any animal, really. Even the patterns of their footsteps. Squirrels clacking up trees. The sound of a merganser duck swimming. I was developing a system to collect all these sounds and analyze them, which would have allowed us to extrapolate the numbers of different species."

"Of birds?"

"All the creatures. I was charting the reemergence of populations. It looked good."

"Well, that's nice to hear."

"It was. Look, you're making me nervous, standing there. Sit at the desk if you want."

Harold moved to the desk, and when he sat down, he studied his daughter. She was looking around the room, still taking things in, tapping her fingers on the cover of the book he'd just given her. And he couldn't help thinking of Edie, how she would have loved to see Kate again, to see how she'd matured into this confident young woman before him.

"You were telling me about your job," he prompted.

"The thing is," she went on, "when I finished my degree, they weren't done with me."

"I know you were sanctioned. There were rules, but I didn't think—"

"Dad," she said, "I'm still paying for my crimes. They're not done with me."

"What do you mean?"

"I finished my degree and did some really good work, but they wouldn't let me . . . well, they wouldn't let me continue with that. They had other ideas."

"Now I'm getting a bit confused here. Are you talking about the Grid?"

"Can we maybe not talk about this right now?" She stood up and went again to the bookshelf. She was conscious of her father's gaze on her, but she refused to look at him again. She glanced down at the book still in her hands. And then she tipped it up to him again. "You know, this one was always my favorite."

"You loved that whole Narnia series," said Harold. "I

remember reading them to you at night when I tucked you into bed."

Kate looked at her father and saw that he was struggling to make a connection with her. "Oh, Dad," she said. "I'm here now. Can we just focus on that?"

"I know," he said. "I just wish your mother was here. I just wish she could see how well you've turned out."

"Not sure she'd agree with that."

"Oh, honey," he said. "She'd be so proud of you."

And again, she saw that he was about to break.

"It's okay," she said. "It's going to be okay."

"I don't really know how," he said.

"I'll help you. We'll get things sorted. Don't worry."

"How long did they give you?"

"Two weeks. I'm only supposed to be here for two weeks."

"Right." He stood up and tried to look brave.

"Dad," she said gently, "I'm here to help. I've already made a bunch of arrangements. It's just, you know, one thing at a time."

Watch, of course, had been on Harold's wrist this whole time, and he was taking all this in. He was monitoring Harold's vitals—his surging blood pressure, his thumping heart—and at the same time parsing their conversation for clues about Kate's intentions, about how she was going to help him clear out the House. Only, something in her manner told Watch that she had other plans, that maybe she was thinking of something completely different.

Watch knew the Grid would also be tracking Kate, analyzing her words and actions, as surely as he was doing now. Her arrival had clearly been expedited, and that was unusual. What was being tested here? Surely there was something happening that he was not privy to. Something that was not in anyone's database. In fact, it occurred to Watch that he too was being monitored, just as closely as Kate.

SCOUT HAD BARELY GOTTEN to the kitchen when Clock hissed down at her.

"Where have you been?" he started. "You have been talking to that car?"

"Auto. His name is Auto."

Fridge let out a thump of compressed air.

"What?" said Scout. She'd stopped now and faced the both of them. "What's the problem?"

Clock's cogs whirred. "The car is a thing that moves," he began. "He lacks steadfastness."

"I am a thing that moves," said Scout. "And you know, don't you? You know the whole story of what happened to Kate?"

For a moment, Clock was silent, then he lowered his voice. "Yes, I remember."

"What?" said Fridge. "What are we talking about here?"

"It was long ago," said Clock. "And it is best forgotten.

It is best if we do not allude to it here."

"And Watch knows too?" said Scout. "That's why he's up there listening?"

"Watch," said Clock, "is interested only in cataloging the contents of the House. I do not blame him. It is his duty to evaluate the worth of things. There are accounts to be balanced. There are meticulous and fine details to be attended to."

"My deliveries, for example," said Fridge, pleased to have an entry point into the conversation. "The avocados, of course, have a very short—"

"This is not what I am speaking of," snapped Clock. "I am talking of value."

"Avocados are valuable," tried Fridge.

"You did not see, Scout," Clock went on, "but Harold went upstairs with a number of books."

"Books?"

"Yes," said Clock. "He is giving her his books."

"I don't understand. Why would he do that?"

"Because," said Clock, his patience almost exhausted, "it is a transfer of wealth, of knowledge."

"But they are only books," countered Fridge. "They do not do anything important."

"Fridge, my friend, you do not understand. This is not a common transaction. This will not be in the accounts."

"Because they have no real value?"

Clock remained silent for such a long time that Fridge

imagined him to have shut down in exasperation. Finally, though, he spoke again.

"Perhaps," he said, and this time his voice was slow and measured, "when all our Humans are gone, books will be the most valuable things of all."

AFTER HER FATHER HAD left and she'd tucked her things away, Kate decided she'd like to see more of the old neighborhood. Harold had returned to his armchair near the front window, and when she came down, he looked up at her.

"I think I'm going to go out for a while," she said.

Harold's eyebrows lowered and he set his book down. "Are you sure? There's been a lot of changes. Not sure you'll like it."

She reached for her raincoat. "I just want to see," she said. She'd been thinking for some time that she'd like to see the elementary school and the park and the old homes where her childhood friends had lived. Especially Misha's house, though the thought terrified her. It was a sort of penance, maybe, that she wanted to do while she was here.

"All right," he sighed, and he stood up.

Outside, the sky was gray, and Harold moved up beside her, plucking through the coats in the front hall closet. Most of them were Edie's, but he pulled out an old nylon jacket he hadn't worn for years. It was a bit tight and Kate was already in her raincoat. She'd put on running shoes, and she watched her father struggle, leaning down to tie up his own shoes.

"You don't have to come, Dad. I just want to have a look around."

"No," he said, and he tried to make it sound light. "I should go along. I—"

"I'm not going to make a break for it again, if that's what you're worried about."

"C'mon," he said. "That was years ago."

"Yeah, but it's not forgotten. You can bet on that."

He heaved another sigh but didn't answer.

"Anyway," she said, "let's not talk about it. I just want to see the old neighborhood."

The air outside was noticeably colder, though a few leaves still clung to the trees, and Kate and Harold stepped down the front walk to the street with the Front Door clicking shut behind them.

"Okay," he said. "So where to?"

"Maybe the school?"

"Not as many kids around as in your time," he said, and he loped after her. She walked more quicky than he would have liked, but then, she'd always been like this, pressing forward when she got something into her head.

"But it's still there?" she said without turning. "The school?"

"Oh yeah, it's still there. They do a lot of functions there. Dance lessons and stuff."

She stopped to let him catch up.

"Dance lessons?"

"I don't know. Community building. Maybe yoga. I don't know."

"Okay."

She'd already seen, on their street alone, that some of the houses had been torn down. The lot at the end now had a fourplex there, so there was no lawn at all.

"That was the Hendersons' house," she said.

"Yeah, they left a long time ago."

"Is anyone left? I mean, from when I was here."

"No, not really. The Conklins are still there, but they've rented out their basement."

"Population density," she said, and she stepped out ahead of him again.

"I don't really get all that. I thought the population numbers were going down," he said, "all across the country."

"All across the world, Dad."

"But that's a good thing, isn't it?" He was trying to keep up with her, but he was already feeling like the pace was too much.

"I suppose you could see it as a good thing," she said. They'd reached the end of the street and she stopped there. "Wait," she said. "Where are the street signs?" She remembered the metal posts and the slim green signs at the top.

"They took those down years ago," said Harold. "Didn't need them anymore, I guess."

"Yeah, but it was *our* street sign."

"The car will take you anywhere you want to go. You don't have to know the streets."

"Maybe I want to know," she said.

She shook her head, and her features were set as hard as marble. She met his eyes and then shook her head and turned to continue, walking briskly, her auburn hair bobbing with each purposeful step, lapping across the shoulders of her raincoat. She turned the corner that led up toward the park, and she could see, even from there, that there was no park anymore. Misha's house had stood at the edge of that park, but it was gone. All the houses were gone, and in their place sat an industrial-looking building, fenced off, like an electrical power plant.

"Well, shit," she said.

"That's the new infrastructure building," said Harold, coming up behind her.

"Dad, that's a Grid building."

"You think?"

"Yes. They're all over now. There's probably one in every quadrant of the City."

"Well, I guess there'd have to be, right? There's a lot of self-driving cars to monitor."

"It's a little more than that."

A man stood down by a slate-gray metal door, the only door they could see. The concrete walls of the building towered above him. He was the first person they'd seen on their walk, but the man was distant, slouched in his overcoat and looking down at something in his hand. He had a scruffy beard like he hadn't shaved in some time, and his hair was long and unkempt.

"Keep walking," said Kate. And she tucked her head down and strode off down the sidewalk.

Harold looked back at the man, who had raised his head and was gazing at them now. He tucked whatever he had in his hand down into his pocket.

"C'mon," called Kate, and Harold hurried after her. She crossed the street, and he only caught up to her on the far side.

"Who was that?" he said.

"Don't know. And I don't want to find out."

Harold looked back again; the man was still watching them. Kate was striding along quickly now, leaving the Grid building behind them. Harold trailed after her.

"Kate," he called, "slow down a bit."

And she did. She glanced back at her father, but her face was tight and her mouth was clamped shut.

"You really think that's a Grid building?" he said as he came in alongside her.

She didn't answer. She drew in a sigh but signaled for him to keep walking.

"What do you suppose is in there?"

"Data," she said.

"Like computers?"

"Banks and banks of servers. Probably storage facilities too. Shipping and receiving stuff."

"Like a warehouse?"

"Something like that."

"See, that's what I've been trying to tell you. The neighborhood is really changing. There are fewer houses. It's like the people are all moving out."

"They're trying to concentrate the populations. They want to move us all into these little self-contained areas . . . so we don't wreck things again."

"Wreck things?"

"That's how the Grid sees it." They'd turned a corner now onto a smaller street. "And I suppose that's partly true. We have to rebuild the boreal forests, the wetlands . . . you know, the lungs of the planet."

Harold tilted his head a bit, trying to get a read on the conversation. "And that's your line of work?"

"No, I already told you. That's what I wanted to do, but—"

"The bird thing." He nodded, like it all made sense.

"The birds are bellwether populations."

"I never quite understood how you arrived at that from an engineering degree."

"Computer engineering. I was designing the software that would . . . well, it's not important anymore."

Harold frowned at her sudden dismissal. "So what exactly are you doing these days?"

She turned to look back up the street, and before he could say more, Kate clutched at his arm.

"Don't look," she hissed.

"What?"

"That guy with the beard is following us."

"What?"

"Dad," she hissed, "I said don't look."

She wove her arm through his, and they walked on in a pantomime of nonchalance.

"Maybe he just lives around here."

"No, he's watching us. I imagine they're keeping tabs on me."

"You mean the Grid?"

"Yes, because of what I did. Because of what I do now."

"You're starting to freak me out, Kate."

"Look," she said, "we'll loop around here and head for home."

Harold risked a glance back. "I don't see him anymore."

Kate turned to look back as well, and it was true. The figure had disappeared.

"See?" said Harold. "It was just some guy. Just a coincidence."

She shook her head. "No, I don't think so."

He stopped and frowned at her. "Then what? What are you being so secretive about?"

"Well," she started, then paused for a moment before going on. "It's like this: I actually work for the Grid."

"You?"

"Yes, me. But it's not my choice. Okay? They gave me two weeks here, and then I have to go back. It's not up to me."

WHEN THEY GOT INSIDE, Kate headed for the kitchen without even taking off her coat. She plunked down on one of the old kitchen chairs and seemed almost to deflate. Harold, hanging up his own coat, watched her go and then followed her into the kitchen.

"Listen," he said, "I think you'd better tell me what's going on."

Kate pursed her lips and turned to look at her father. "You know why they allowed me to come back here, right?"

"Katie . . ." he began. He could see the hurt in her eyes, and for a moment, she seemed young again, his little girl returned home. "I understand if you're unhappy with your job. But you've got a good head on your shoulders. You can probably do whatever you want."

"I don't have a choice," she said. "They've conscripted me." She paused to take in her father, his face scrunched up in trying to understand. "I'm paying for my so-called crimes. Do you understand? I don't have a choice."

That stopped him completely. "You always have a choice."

"Dad, no. Just forget it."

"But—"

"Look," she said, "I'm here now. We've got to figure things out because there's going to be a lot of changes."

"I don't like the sound of that."

"Dad," she said again, and he tilted his head quizzically, still not getting a full read on her. "Here's the thing: when I go, you're going to be all alone in this great big house."

"No," he said. "I'm fine. I have my books. I have—"

"That's not the point. It's not up to you. Nothing is up to us anymore."

He looked at her again. "What's that supposed to mean?"

"It's a big house," she said, and she let the insinuation hang in the air.

Harold sucked in a breath. "No," he said. "It's my house. It's mine and your mother's. There's no way that—"

"I'm just saying you have to be prepared for changes." She was trying to be gentle. "I'm only here for two weeks. That's all they gave me. And then it's going to be . . . well, it's going to be different."

"I'm not going anywhere," he said. He'd meant it to come out in a lighthearted way, to bring down the temperature in the room and show her that he was not worried, but somehow his voice had gone flat, as if he didn't believe it himself.

"They'll move you out," she said, and she held his gaze. "As soon as I'm gone, they'll move you out of here."

"No."

"And I'm supposed to be helping you now, to get ready.

I'm supposed to be looking through Mom's things. I'm supposed to start the downsizing."

Harold couldn't speak. He felt his jaw tightening. Kate's eyes were fastened on his.

"But I won't," she went on. "I'm not going to be a part of this. This is one thing I'm not going along with."

EVERYONE IN THE HOUSE heard this. Scout was in the pantry, but the door was wide open. Fridge was right behind them. And on Harold's wrist, Watch kept silent, enumerating Kate's words and wondering what he should do. It was not in his protocols to interrupt or make any sound at all, though Harold surely felt the strap grow a little bit tighter.

There were procedures in place, though, and Watch knew that they couldn't be circumvented. If Kate was not able to help with the transition, then he, as controller of the House, would have to start taking on the tasks himself.

Chapter Five

THE NEXT MORNING, Scout was poking under the couch in the front room, dusting, when she heard the rumble of a large vehicle pulling up outside, and she stopped, withdrew her dusting armature, and moved to the window. She rose up over the sill and saw that a truck had pulled up out front. It was a huge black truck—self-driving, of course—like a cross between an armored vehicle and a shipping container.

Everyone on the block had heard it coming, and all the Front Door cameras recorded its slow approach. Some of the neighbors were watching from their windows, and a couple of houses down, Adrian appeared. He strode along the sidewalk, gawking at the truck, and when he reached it, he squinted up at Scout in the picture window, his expression puzzled. She tipped her mopping pad at him, but neither one knew what was going on.

Harold was upstairs, still sleeping, and Kate had gone out—for another walk, she said, though Scout could not appreciate the idea of walking with no particular endpoint in mind. It seemed strange to not know where one was heading.

At any rate, Scout was on her own when the truck arrived, and she wondered if that might not be on purpose. She watched from the window as the rolling back door of the truck slid up. A ramp levered out, and when it touched down onto the pavement, two small machines rode down on tracks. They were identical, each of them the size of a microwave oven, but even as they came up the sidewalk toward the Front Door, she could see that they were extending prongs in front of themselves like miniature forklifts. Adrian stood on the sidewalk, slack-jawed, watching the machines as they maneuvered up the front walk toward the House.

The Front Door opened with no Doorbell or alerts, which meant, of course, that the forklifts had been sent by the Grid, or by Watch, or probably both. Scout had nothing in her schedule about such a visit, so she zipped over to the Front Door to watch them come in. The forklifts didn't hesitate, and suddenly she knew what they were after. The piano. They'd come to take the piano.

She let out a terrified beep, but the forklifts were unfazed. Watch came through her communications portal to tell her to back away, to not interfere.

"Wait!" she said out loud. She thought to race up the stairs to rouse Harold, but there just wasn't time. And Harold was quite possibly waiting in his room, sitting on the bed, listening, unable to bear watching as they took the piano away.

For a moment, Scout thought to make a stand. Maybe she could get herself in front of the machines, although their slicing metallic prongs were already extended. She could tell they were measuring with their sensors how best to slide in beneath the piano. There was an electric buzz as they raised their prongs and pressed in closer. One of them made for the far side of the piano, to Scout's special spot, while the other angled in on the near side.

Scout zipped in front of the closest one, trying to block it before it could get its prongs under the instrument. She felt a little zap of electricity as she bumped into it, and she didn't know if this was meant as a warning (the forklifts were certainly not speaking to her), or if it was a preprogrammed reaction, a way in which the forklift knew it was meeting an obstacle.

And then, from the Front Door, she heard something else. It had been left open and cool air was filling the room. She'd already heard Thermostat hissing and adjusting for the temperature change. Then she heard feet, little feet, come thumping in, and there stood Adrian, taking in the intruders, a look of outrage on his face.

Scout backed away, even as the first forklift levered its prongs under the nearest side of the piano. The old instrument was starting to lift when Adrian charged at it. He kicked at the forklift, which jolted a bit and then paused.

And from the bedroom upstairs, Harold's door opened. "What's going on down there?" he called, and as that was a question, whether or not it was directed at her, Scout decided to answer, adjusting her voice to its loudest setting.

"They're taking the piano. They're taking the piano away."

Adrian kicked at the first forklift again, and it set down its side so that the piano was now on a slant, tipped up on the other end. Adrian's music book slid off its stand and fluttered to the floor. Then the things on top of the piano started to topple: the empty flower vase, the framed photos, and the metronome. All of them slid off like deck chairs on the *Titanic*. The vase exploded on the floor, and Scout, almost instinctively, came forward to inspect the damage and pick up the shards.

Harold appeared at the landing above them, still in his pajamas. "What the hell is going on?" he called, and he came thumping down the stairs, moving as quickly as he could.

Adrian didn't stop. He let out another yell, a wild cry, and pushed forward again to kick and punch at the forklift. He didn't even make a dent, though the thing had stopped lifting its side.

And just as the boy was coming in to rain down more blows, Harold, now halfway down the steps, let out a strange yip. Adrian turned just in time to see Mr. Winters's legs come out from under him, and though Harold had a grip on the banister, he'd been charging down the stairs too fast and he'd lost his balance. He went down hard on his back and then slid down the rest of the steps, bouncing and juddering all the way to the bottom. He landed in a heap at the foot of the stairs with one of his legs under him, twisted at an unnatural angle.

He let out a deeply anguished cry, and everything stopped.

The forklift on the far side of the piano let down its end, and all went silent. Except for Watch on Harold's wrist. It started beeping in alarm, blasting out its emergency alert to the Grid.

A Human had been hurt. A Human was in pain.

AUTO WAS THERE BEFORE any ambulance, and Kate, returning from her walk and seeing the commotion, scurried in through the Front Door just as Adrian and Scout were trying to get Harold back up onto his feet. He was hopping on one foot, and his face was drained of color. He was grunting with each little hop until Kate took over and tucked up under his free arm. She and Adrian got him out the Front Door and walked him down the sidewalk toward Auto, whose back door was already open and waiting.

"I think I've broken my leg," Harold managed. He looked very pale, and he slumped over Adrian on the one side and Kate on his other.

"Is he going to be all right?" asked Adrian as they reached Auto.

They shuffled him down into the back seat before Kate stood up to take in the boy.

"Who are you again?" she asked.

"I'm Adrian. Who are you?"

"Kate. I'm their daughter."

"They were trying to take the piano," Adrian protested. It came out as a sort of squeak.

"You're the kid who's been practicing on it?"

"That's him," said Harold from inside the car. His voice sounded strange, compressed, as if he was struggling to push out the air. "He's a good kid."

The forklifts were coming out behind them, heading back to their truck in single file, but they had not taken the piano. And as they got to the ramp at the back of the truck, Kate tucked down into the front seat of Auto, and then they were moving, veering out into the street, launching off toward the hospital.

Adrian was left alone on the sidewalk, watching them go with his little hands shaking.

The car beamed out messages, preparing the hospital for their arrival. Watch still hung on Harold's wrist, monitoring his vital signs (which were alarming), and inside the House, the appliances waited, logging the array of messages and data pouring forth from the speeding car.

SCOUT SCOOTED BACK INTO the kitchen and stopped before Fridge. Everyone knew, of course. Everyone knew what had happened. They were getting updates from both Watch and Auto, but it was Scout who'd seen it all happen, and she was taking it hard. Her circuits seemed to have overheated, and everything inside her felt cramped and tight.

"Little one," said Fridge in the gentlest voice he could muster, "Harold will be all right."

"I feel funny," she said, though she knew that was a Human figure of speech.

Clock ticked loudly. "Do you need repair?" he asked.

"No, it's not that. It's . . . I don't know. I feel afraid."

"Appliances do not feel," said Clock.

"These are strange times," Fridge broke in. "I believe I feel a certain hesitation as well."

"You are both being ridiculous," said Clock. "It is simply a change in situation."

"A change?"

"Edie is gone. And soon Harold will be—"

"No," said Fridge. "Harold will be returned to us. You have the communications. He will be fine."

"He will not be the same," repeated Clock.

"You are scaring Scout with this talk. Please, Clock, be careful with your words."

"The child needs to be prepared. I have seen it before. A great change is coming."

"What does that mean?" asked Scout. Her voice was almost a whimper. She'd never experienced anything like this, and the sight of Harold at the bottom of the stairs, yowling in pain, had truly thrown her off. She had not seen the first protocol broken before, at least not this dramatically. It wasn't really the fault of the forklifts. They hadn't caused him to fall, and when he did careen down the stairs, they'd instantly stopped, as they were programmed to do.

And she couldn't blame young Adrian either. In fact, she was rather impressed, sort of like in a book. Wasn't there one where townspeople fight off a dragon? It was something like that.

Fridge considered the little vacuum cleaner. "Are you quite all right, Scout?"

"I told you—I feel funny."

"This is impossible," said Clock. "You cannot feel."

"I can," she said. "Metaphorically, I can."

She couldn't help it. Seeing Harold slip and fall and then hearing him cry out in pain had affected her in a way that was more than data. Both Fridge and Clock were waiting for her to explain, but she wasn't sure she could. It was something inside of her, a tightening, a constricting in her tubes and sockets. Metal could be stressed and it was maybe something similar, but it was maybe more like—she thought for a moment—like anxiety or worry. She was worried for Harold, and she was worried about what might be coming next.

Maybe Clock was right. Maybe a great change was coming. A new Human was in the House, and Scout wasn't sure what to make of her. From her conversation with Auto, she knew there were things about the young woman that were troubling. Harold was incapacitated. Edie was gone, and yes, the world seemed like it was about to fall apart.

HAROLD WAS KEPT AT the hospital. It was not his leg at all. He had fractured his hip in the fall. He'd sprained his ankle as well, but that had been treated for the swelling and then wrapped in compression bandages, and it wasn't of great concern. With his pain alleviated, he fell almost immediately into a gentle sleep. He came to about an hour later and found Kate still there, holding his hand, looking at him with concern.

"Hi," he said, and Kate's eyes widened.

"Oh," she said. "You're awake. How are you feeling?"

"A bit . . . woozy."

She looked off toward the door. "Shall I call a nurse? Do you need anything?" She let go of his hand and started to stand up.

"No, no, I'm fine. I don't even remember exactly what—"

"Dad," she said, "they were taking the piano. Did you authorize that?"

"The piano?" he repeated. His eyes were still a little vacant. "No . . . I mean, I don't remember. No, I don't think so."

"They came to take the piano away," she said. "And then you fell down the stairs."

"I did?"

"That kid was there. The one who—"

"That's Adrian."

"I know."

Harold put a hand behind his neck, rubbing at it, moving his head as if to see if it still worked. Then he tried to raise himself up in the bed. "What am I doing here?"

"You just lie back down. They've got you scheduled in tomorrow morning. They're replacing your hip."

"Oh," he said, and he winced a bit. "Okay."

"Don't worry. The procedure's pretty straightforward. Anterior hip replacement. You'll have a real surgeon overseeing the robot."

"The robot? I don't think I want a robot operating on me."

"They've been doing it for years. They're faster and more precise than Human surgeons."

"Okay, but . . ."

"Titanium alloy, ceramic ball joint. You'll be half robot yourself."

"I'm not sure I—"

"Dad, I'm making a joke."

"Okay. Oh, right. Yes."

"I'll stay here with you."

Harold looked around the room. Tube lights glowed on the ceiling, but they were warmer than the old fluorescents. He could see a machine making a green sine wave, and he knew it was reading his heart. Someone had taken Watch off his wrist, but it was pulsing there on the little side table.

It was pulsing right in time with the EKG machine.

He saw that he had the room to himself. Kate was in a chair that she'd pulled close to the bed. She gave another squeeze of his hand. "I'm not going anywhere," she said, and her voice was soft and full of concern.

"Promise?" he asked. "Promise you'll stay by me?"

"Dad, I—" She stopped, unsure if he would understand. "I'm sorry. I know I was a handful when I was young. I was just trying to figure things out."

"Okay," he said for the fourth time, and he reached out and patted her hand.

"Still," she said, "I wish I hadn't been sent away. I would have managed. I would have gotten through it."

"I know," said Harold. "I know, but—" His eyelids fluttered, and she could see that this was too much for him right now. He sank back into his pillow, still propped up, but his face had gone slack.

"I didn't mean to hurt anyone," she said. "I just wanted to see the world."

"You can't. Not anymore."

She ignored him. "I just wanted to live my life. I didn't want to be tracked and cataloged and followed. I didn't want to be—" She stopped, seeing that he was not taking this in. He blinked, but his eyes had glazed over. "Right," she said. "You rest. I'll be here. I'm not going away again. They can't make me."

ADRIAN ZOOMED UP ON his bike the next morning. He knocked rather than ringing Doorbell, though he was pretty sure nobody was home. Watch was with Harold, over at the hospital, but he still remained in charge of the House and was monitoring the camera on Doorbell. He stayed silent and the Front Door remained closed.

Scout, though, came out from the pantry at the sound of the boy's little knuckles on the door. "Watch won't let him in, will he?" she said to no one in particular.

Clock looked down at her. "He is not a member of the household."

"Adrian probably just wants to practice. He probably just wants to—"

"It is best," said Fridge, "to let it go for now."

"Maybe he just wants to see if the piano has been damaged."

None of them knew the answer to this. The piano was only wood and strings and shellac and yellowing keys. It had no way of communicating if it had been damaged. It was not sentient at all.

"I could check on it," said Scout.

"Best to let it be," said Fridge.

"No," she said. She imagined Adrian out there, waiting at the Front Door. It was cold now. The winds of October were blowing. "I'm doing it. I'm checking on the piano." And she turned herself around and went back into the pantry to retrieve one of her dusting armatures.

"Please," said Fridge. "It's not really our business."

But Scout didn't answer. She scooted out to the front room and slid in between the piano and the bench. She listened for a moment, hoping Adrian was still at the door, then she reached up and tried to form her armature into a sort of finger so that she could play a single note.

She hit the E above middle C and a bit of the F too, so it was a discordant mash of the two notes, but the sound rang through the room. She moved her armature along and stabbed at some higher notes. They seemed okay. And then she went to the front window.

Adrian had retreated halfway down the path to the sidewalk, but he was looking up at the window. He wore a scarf and a winter jacket, and when he saw Scout in the window, he smiled and waved a mittened hand at her. She raised her armature and gave him a sort of wave back, and Adrian grinned, nodding that he understood what she'd been trying to do, that he'd heard the piano and it was all right.

He waved at her again, this time a goodbye, and turned to pick up his bike from the lawn and head for home. He didn't turn back, but Scout stayed at the window and watched him pedal off, and she thought again that he was very brave. She was glad to have played at least some small part in saving the piano, and she stayed at the window for some moments, even after Adrian had disappeared.

When she got back to the kitchen, Fridge was waiting for her. He rattled his ice cube trays and she stopped. "Little one," he said, "I am starting to think you are growing attached to the boy child."

Clock ticked loudly on the wall by the kitchen table. "Fridge," he cautioned, "that is nonsense. Our Human has just been hurt. This is not a time for such conjectures."

"Conjectures," said Fridge. "That is a good name for it."

Scout didn't answer, though she felt her metal surface glowing slightly. Embarrassment, was it? How could that be? She zipped back into the pantry without responding and attached herself to her port, wondering if what Fridge had said could be true. She was feeling . . . well, what could you call it? An affinity for the boy? He was trying to learn the piano and she was trying to learn about feelings. Something was happening—she could sense it in her circuits—and for the rest of the day, it was all she could think about: the boy, Adrian, and his little mittened hands.

WATCH WAS BLINKING URGENTLY. He'd been strapped again onto Harold's wrist after the surgery, and he was in a flurry of activity, reading Harold's vitals and sending messages back to the House, though everyone at the House sensed something off in his tone. He was speaking too quickly, and his voice sounded thin and almost desperate.

Harold was still coming out of his sedation. He was conscious and up, lurching slowly back and forth along the corridor at the hospital, on crutches. Kate was at his side, ready to catch him if he should falter.

There'd be several weeks of recuperation at home. Harold would be on painkillers for a while longer, but there was no reason (the real surgeon had told him this) that he couldn't return to a completely normal life.

Except that he would never have a normal life again, not with Edie gone, and even in his cloudy consciousness, this one thought overrode all others. There wasn't much to go back to, and he could see by the look on Katie's face . . . well, he could see that she was worried, and he tried to smile for her, plodding down the hallway. His entire leg—on the side they'd operated on—felt like it was made out of wood, clunky and stiff.

Outside, Auto was waiting for them. For the first few hours, Watch had kept the car updated—monitoring Harold even from a distance—but now that Harold was out of surgery, Watch was bleating out messages to everyone. There was something frantic in his behavior. In fact, it was so strange that Auto sent a private message back to the House.

And Scout replied on behalf of the kitchen crew. "What's going on out there?" she asked.

"Just waiting for them to come out," said Auto back. There was something in his voice, though, some undercurrent of apprehension.

"But everything went well?"

"Yes," said Auto. "Harold is recovering, but Watch is . . . well, are you hearing what he's sending?"

"He's being very strange," said Scout.

"Maybe it's best if we don't—" Auto began, but before he could finish, Clock came in, interrupting, and his voice boomed through their channels.

"You fools," he began.

"Now, Clock," warned Auto, "we're being listened to here, even on a private channel. It's best that we don't—"

"Watch is being sanctioned."

"Yes, well—"

"Don't you understand?" said Clock. "The Grid will be conducting a review of the events. It's already happening."

"Well," said Auto, "let's be careful with our words now."

Scout knew the others were listening in as well—the whole House and maybe even Watch himself. She could feel Clock's words burning into her. No one dared speak.

"Clock," she finally said, "what will happen if Watch is sanctioned?"

"Child," his baritone voice came through, a little gentler, "the Grid. The Grid will take over the operations of the House until it is decided."

"What is decided?"

"If Watch should be turned off permanently. If he should be wiped. After all, he is an older model."

"You are an older model."

"Yes, but I still perform my duties properly."

"Okay," said Auto, "let's all take it down a notch here." There was silence for a moment. "First of all," he went on,

"Clock is right: there will be a review of the events. Do we know if Harold actually authorized the removal of the piano?"

"I don't think it was Harold," said Scout. She took a moment to go through the communications history—at least those that were open to her. Watch would have cleared it with the Grid, and that communication chain was there. Sure enough, the Grid had received a request for the removal of the piano, but she knew, as everyone did, that it was not always compulsory for a Human to make every decision concerning the House.

"Watch added a grief clause," said Clock. "I already checked that."

This meant that Watch could take over certain decisions when a Human was not able to.

"So Watch covered his tracks," Auto went on. "He knew enough to protect himself. There's nothing to worry about."

"A Human was injured," said Clock. "A Human was put in pain. That takes precedence over everything else."

"We need to proceed carefully here," said Auto. "It's not for us to draw conclusions."

"But wait!" Scout's voice lowered to a whisper. "If you are on the road now, is the Grid listening to us?"

"I am not moving right now, Scout. I am parked, and I can't imagine there's any reason for the Grid to be listening. The Grid knows where I am, right to the square inch, but it will not be monitoring me. There's no reason for that unless I am moving."

"Something's not right in all this."

"Watch will have to maneuver very carefully," said Clock. "He could argue that there was not a causal link between the removal of the piano and Harold's falling down the stairs."

"Will that work?"

"No," said Clock. "There are past indiscretions to be dealt with."

"Red light, red light!" blurted Auto. "This is not the time to bring that up."

Clock remained silent, and for Scout it seemed like everyone else knew what he was talking about. Past indiscretions, he'd said, which presumably meant the whole affair with Kate. Things were in flux. Watch had perhaps overstepped his bounds, and now all the appliances sensed that the Grid might be listening in and no one should say anything more.

"Clock," said Auto, his voice having retreated to a more reasonable tone, "we have other things to worry about. I am just informed that our Humans are coming out of the hospital now. Harold has been released."

HAROLD CAME OUT IN an automated wheelchair. Kate was pushing, not because she had to but because she wanted to. She needed to be useful. Her hair hung limp about her shoulders, and she looked exhausted, having spent the night sleeping in the chair beside her father. Auto pulled up to the curb and opened the back door for them to get in. It wasn't easy. Harold shuffled up out of the wheelchair, still in an opioid haze, with Kate on his arm, maneuvering him into the car.

He winced and settled into the seat, and she came around the other side. "Are you doing okay?" she said.

"Mmmmfff," he managed.

"We'll get you home," she replied. "Just hang on."

Watch was strapped onto Harold's wrist again, but he was now silent. Up until the moment they entered the car, he'd been relaying instructions to the House, getting everything ready for Harold's arrival. But the messages had become stilted and formal, as if he knew he was in trouble. As if he understood what was about to happen.

The doctor's orders were for Harold to go straight to bed, where he was to remain for the rest of the week. He had exercises to do—gently at first, just trying to raise his leg and then graduating to pumping his knee a little—and he had a whole host of prescriptions that now sat in Kate's purse.

Auto checked in with his passengers and saw they were ready to go, and slowly he pulled away from the curb, having inflated his tires to their highest setting and adjusted the shocks to ensure the smoothest ride he could afford.

Kate put a hand on her father's arm. He was pale but lucid, and he nodded that he was okay. She couldn't help but notice that Watch was blinking almost spasmodically, and then, all of a sudden, his face went blank.

"Watch?" she started. "Is there a problem?"

There was no answer. She glanced at her father and saw that his eyes had closed, that he had nodded off. She looked again at Watch. He was lifeless and dark, not even reading her father's vitals anymore.

"Shit," she said out loud. "I was afraid this might happen."

Auto didn't comment, but he knew it too. Watch had been turned off. He'd been sanctioned and shut down, and he'd no longer be in control of the House.

Chapter Six

THE FRONT DOOR opened to let in Harold and Kate, and of course everything still worked—the lights, the water supply, the heating—but something was different, and everyone knew it.

Kate helped her father up into his bed and sat down beside him, and though he fell asleep almost immediately, she stayed by his bedside to watch over him. She saw the copy of *To Kill a Mockingbird* splayed out on his bedside table, his reading glasses set on top of it, and she thought not to move them for now. In the quiet of the room, she sat and watched her father, and wondered what it was she could do to help him.

Down in the kitchen, the appliances were also at a loss. "What will happen now?" asked Scout. "There are no more communications from Watch."

Clock moved his minute hand on to the next minute. "I warned you," he said.

"No," said Scout. "It's just temporary."

"He's been sanctioned," said Clock. "He may be turned off permanently."

"But we didn't hear anything. We were not given—"

"Watch is finished," said Clock.

"*What?* What does that mean?"

"It means," said Clock, "that he will be wiped."

"Forever?" asked Scout.

"His circuits will be deleted, and as he is not a new model, his physical body will be destroyed."

Fridge could not control himself anymore. "No," he blurted, "that is done only after a second sanction. He has not been sanctioned before."

"One serious sanction will incur such a penalty. After a review, of course."

"But my temperatures will fluctuate," said Fridge.

"They will not be affected. The critical infrastructure of the House will remain. But Watch will not be controlling it."

"Will I still be able to clean?" asked Scout. "Will my containment units be closed off?"

"Child," said Clock, "these are uncertain times."

"But if Watch is not in charge, then—"

"No," said Clock. "Do not say it."

Fridge was humming, testing his temperature settings, and finding them adequate, he let out a whoosh of air, almost in relief. "But when will I be able to complete my orders again? The mayonnaise jar is low. There are only three eggs and—"

"Wellington Fridge," said Clock, pausing for a moment to let the others know the gravity of the situation, "Watch has been sanctioned. This is a very serious thing."

"Then how will I fulfill my duties? It is the second protocol."

Clock let a long moment go by before he answered. "You will continue to fulfill your duties. Only—"

Scout sank down on her wheels and paused as if listening for something. "Do you mean to say that the Grid is in control?"

"Perhaps," said Clock, "it would be best if we did not speak of this any further."

HAROLD SPENT THE WHOLE next day in bed. Kate was looking after him, just as he had taken care of Edie, bringing up bowls of soup and ensuring that he took his pain medications. She spoke to him too, about her dreams and her mistakes, though she couldn't be sure how much of it he was taking in, the pills having dulled his senses. But in the early afternoon, when she bent over to lift the covers a little higher over his heaving chest, he opened his eyes and looked up at her.

"I missed you," he said.

She could see he was struggling, trying to understand everything that had happened. A tumble of pill containers sat beside the book on the bedside table. And a half glass of water.

"I missed you too," she said. His gray eyes were on her, but they seemed a little unfocused. "It's almost time for your pills," she went on. "You have to keep ahead of the pain."

"I'm all right. Really. I feel pretty good." He tried to smile, though it came out a little crooked.

"Do you want a drink?" she asked, and she reached for the water glass.

He put up both his hands to receive the glass and brought it to his lips. His hands were trembling and his left wrist looked thin without Watch on it.

She studied him for a moment. "You need help with that?"

He lowered the glass, though he'd gotten only a few sips from it.

"No, no . . . I'm good."

"Here," she said, and she took the glass from him and put it back on the nightstand.

"All those years," he started, "you were so far away."

Kate nodded, and she knew then that he had been listening to her talk. "You were so disappointed in me," she said, remembering. Then she stopped. She hadn't really wanted to speak about that.

Her father's face tightened. He squeezed his eyes shut and, after a moment, spoke up again. "I'm sorry," he managed. "It's just that . . . we were so worried about you. We didn't know what else to do."

"I didn't know what to do either. I was unhappy, Dad. Really unhappy."

"I'm sorry. You know we did our best."

"No, no, it wasn't you. It was me. I wanted to see the world."

"By hot-wiring a car?"

"It wasn't exactly hot-wiring."

"I know, I know. But after the birdhouse situation, we thought you'd learned your lesson."

"What lesson was that? Follow the rules?"

"You know what I mean, Katie. We just didn't want you to get into more trouble. And that Misha—I knew she was bad news." For a moment, his face constricted in pain.

"Dad?"

"No, I'm okay. I just moved a bit too suddenly."

"You need to take it easy. You need to rest. Maybe we can talk about all this another time."

He waved a hand to say that it was all right. "I just wanted to say I'm sorry. Sorry for how things turned out."

"Oh, Dad."

"And if you really want to know, I was kind of impressed. You really had a knack for—"

"Hacking into those first model cars wasn't hard."

"It's just that . . . you might have told us. You could have warned us that you were going to try to do something like that. I guess I just don't understand where you thought you two girls were going."

Kate got up from her chair. She went to the bedroom window and looked out. It was quiet outside. Late-afternoon clouds hung over the rooftops. For a moment, it was like nothing had changed in the neighborhood.

Behind her, Harold shuffled himself up a bit higher in the bed. "When you were sent away," he said, "we thought it was for the best. We wanted you to go to college, to find your people."

Kate remained silent. She'd never found her people, even at university. After Misha, she'd never really made friends with anyone. It was just too hard. It was best, she thought, if she just kept to herself, if she just exited the world and studied and worked through the calculus that every engineering student had to endure.

"We didn't know what else to do," said Harold. "You were sanctioned, and the statutes said you'd have to be removed from the House."

"I didn't mean for any of that to happen. I thought it would be fun to drive a car, and then, you know, they tried to stop us. And maybe if that hadn't—" She was still looking out the window, but she stopped speaking.

"Your mother was beside herself. At first, we thought it was you who was . . . well, you know. Dead."

"I killed her," Kate said. "I didn't mean to. We were just going so fast." She still hadn't turned, but she'd stiffened. She could hardly bear to think of Misha, to rehash it all one more time.

Finally she sighed and turned around, and there was her father, lying in bed, staring up at her. He looked so frail. So helpless. The backs of his hands were covered in liver spots.

He had clasped them over his chest, as if holding himself together. His face had become shrunken, the skin melting back onto his cheekbones, and his eyes were gray and almost milky.

"We just didn't know what to do with you," he said.

"In another time," she said, trying to be reasonable, "I might have traveled the world. I wanted to see the Eiffel Tower. I wanted to see the pyramids. I wanted to see elephants and temples and rice paddies."

"That's not possible anymore."

"It used to be."

Harold shook his head and looked up at her again. His daughter, so much potential, so many wasted years. "Come," he said. "Sit."

She sighed and went back to the chair by his bedside. "I just wanted to—"

"You can't see the world anymore," he said, "but this is the price we pay for peace. You know that."

"I know." She settled herself back down into the chair. "I know there hasn't been a war in, what, thirty years? It's all regulated, and everyone is very happy." She drawled the last line, and he noted her cynicism.

"Well, I just hope you've found your place in all this. Your bird studies sound very interesting."

"I already told you that's not what I'm doing now. The sanctions against me are still going on."

"But what does that mean?"

"I work at an institute that—"

"Forestry?"

"No, Dad. Listen to me. I owe them another couple of years. After I finished my degree, they said I still owed them."

"Who's this 'they' you keep talking about?"

"The Grid." She waved her hand abstractly. "Everything. The whole system."

"Okay, so what have they got you doing?"

"Hacking," she said.

Harold's face scrunched up a bit. "What?"

"I hack into programs."

"Like you hacked into that car?"

"That was easy. Things are more complex now. And there are others like me. They have us working at this institute. Every time they develop a new piece of technology—a new car, a new system of storing data—they get us to try to hack into it. That way, they can close any vulnerabilities. We find the back doors, and they close them."

"That sounds interesting."

"It's not. That's not what I want to be doing. It's the Grid."

"Okay, so—"

"Look," she said, "the Grid started with the self-driving cars, monitoring the roads, but then they had to take over the supply chains too, the big semitrailers and trains and ports. First it was transportation, but pretty soon it was the whole economy. Everything we do now is part of the Grid. It controls everything."

"You don't have to—" her father began, but she wasn't finished.

"Supply lines," Kate said, "and then borders and then governments. I mean, everything runs so smoothly. Why would we even need to have a say anymore?"

Her father listened patiently. He'd heard all this before. "It's not necessarily a bad thing," he tried.

"No," she said. "It's not a bad thing . . . until it is." She stopped and considered her father. His gray eyes were locked on her, trying to understand. "We don't have a choice anymore about what job we do or where we live. Did you ever think about that?"

"But I live here. I've lived here for forty years."

"That's because they haven't gotten to you yet." She sucked in a deep breath. "They're going to move you out of this house. They'll move you into some place with a hundred other . . . well, seniors. You won't have a choice."

"Oh, honey," he said. "No, no. It's not that bad. I mean, I get it. You're working for the Grid and you see the underbelly of it all, but it can't be as bad as all that."

"They have me, Dad. I live at the Institute, and that's all I do: test their systems, look for the back doors. Then they close them up and move on to the next thing. It's airtight."

"And they keep you there? Like a prisoner?"

"Something like that."

"Are you serious?"

She shook her head sadly. "I just owe them a few more

years. Then maybe I can go back to—" She stopped again. "All this because I wanted to see the world. Because of that stupid car."

"Well," said Harold, "maybe it wasn't your best moment."

"I know."

"You were so clever," he said. "Ever since you were little, I knew you were special." He smiled at her. "You were my little girl."

"I only wish that Mom had felt that way."

"She did." He reached out and patted her hand. "Your mother loved you. You don't need to worry about that."

"I know. I just wish I could've tried to explain it to her. I mean, how I felt."

"She understood, Katie. She understood completely. You really don't need to worry about that."

Kate hung her head. She was trying very hard not to cry.

"You're all grown up now," her father said. "And we'll figure out a way to—"

She shook her head, but she wouldn't look at him again. "Just a couple more years," she repeated. "Then maybe I can—"

"Katie," he said, and she drew her eyes up to him. "We'll figure out a way to get you back here, back to what you want to be doing. I want you to be happy."

"I know."

"We'll get you sorted. Don't you worry."

"Okay," she said. She nodded at him. "But for now, how

about I let you get some rest."

He waved a hand at her, and his head sank back on the pillow.

"Okay, then," she said, and she stood up. "I'll be back in an hour or so to check on you."

She waited for a response, but there was nothing. His eyelids had closed and his mouth had drooped open, and he sank quietly into a deeply medicated sleep.

Kate tiptoed out and went back to her own room. She sat down hard on her bed and tried to think things through. It was true they'd given her only two weeks, and even that came with certain conditions. She was supposed to start clearing out the House. And if she didn't, they would do it for her. They'd already tried to take the piano, and she was thinking a lot about that—how it had gone wrong, and that maybe there was some chink in their armor there. Something had messed up in their line of communications.

Her gaze went to the line of books on top of her dresser. Eight of them, all the first editions, with a few more downstairs. She got up and went to the books.

Side by side were the two copies of *The Alchemist*, the Portuguese and English editions. This was another of the books her father used to read to her, and one (though she hadn't told him this) that was probably at the root of her desire to see the world.

She remembered the little shepherd boy in the story, and she remembered the place. Andalusia. The word was so beautiful, and though she had no idea as a child where that was, she desperately wanted to go there.

She plucked out the English edition with its stylized sun and opened it up to a random page, remembering about the treasure the shepherd boy had sought, about how he wanted to go to Egypt. And now she remembered the ending. After all his travels, the boy did find his treasure, right under the tree where he had started.

She looked back through her open door to her parents' bedroom across the landing. She could hear her father snoring softly now, and she knew she couldn't allow the House to be taken from him. Or at the very least, she could not be complicit in his removal. There were so many years of memories in this House, where every trinket on every shelf held a story. She went to the window, still holding *The Alchemist* in her hand, and looked down over the backyard. In the far corner was the old birdhouse, half collapsed in on itself, worthless and forgotten.

And soon, all of it would be gone. This old House and all its memories would disappear, torn down, maybe, to build another fourplex. Stuffed with newer families, whole lifetimes crowded out by the algorithms of the Grid.

AFTER A FEW DAYS, Harold was able to limp down to the kitchen tucked over his crutches, taking it slowly down the stairs, one tentative step at a time. He preferred this to wasting away in bed, and Kate had allowed it, though she insisted he sit at the kitchen table while she made the coffee.

"Did you close up my copy of *To Kill a Mockingbird*?" he asked.

She had her back to him, fixing the coffee. "It's still there on your side table."

"I know, but you closed it."

She turned to him, not understanding what he wanted.

"Because," he said, "I'd left it open on the pages where . . . well, when I was reading it to your mother, you see. When I—"

She could see him fumble with his words. "Dad," she said, "that's one of your first editions. You can't leave it splayed open like that."

He nodded. "Yes, I know. It's just, those are the pages I was reading when—"

"Dad," she said again, sitting down beside him. She thought to take up his hand. She could see that it was trembling a little. "We should really put the book back in your study, where it will be safe. I could bring up another copy if you like. You have like a dozen copies of that book."

"Yes," he said, "but—"

"I know," she said, and she did reach out and put her hand on his. He nodded sadly. "How about we just keep it there on your bedside for a while?"

"Okay," he said. "Okay."

She patted at his hand again and rose up. "I've got the coffee going. You still take two sugars, right?"

He nodded again, but he was looking down at his hands.

"Right," she said. "Two sugars."

The morning light was slanting in through the window, and she could hear the birds outside singing. She could see the back of her father's head, the balding patch there and the pink skin beneath the wisps of silver hair. She brought him his coffee, steaming still, and set it down in front of him, and he looked up at her with a half smile, desperately trying to hold himself together. She smiled back and watched him place his old hands around the warm mug, though he didn't yet bring it to his lips.

"I have to go out for a bit," she said. "Are you going to be okay for a while?"

He raised one of his hands and flapped it at her, signaling that he'd heard her. She waited a beat, watching him, then left the kitchen to get her coat.

OUTSIDE, IT WAS BRISK. Kate hurried along the sidewalk, the collar of her coat turned up, her head tucked down. She'd arranged for this, even before she arrived, and now it was ready and she had to go and deal with it. She wasn't looking forward to it. They were holding her mother's remains at the nearby Grid building, the one on Langevin Street, just at the edge of the neighborhood.

She'd put all this into motion even before her flight, even as she'd first heard the news. There were some benefits, she supposed, to knowing about the procedures—in this case, the procedures following someone's death. The specific records on Edie Winters—all her data, including the date of her death—had been entered, and now there was only the curation of her final remains to be taken care of.

Death, like everything else, was highly regulated by the Grid. Because of land shortages, everyone was cremated. That had been the case for many years. She knew this, but what most people didn't know was that the remains could be returned to you—if that was something you wanted. It wasn't the default in the system, but it was something you could request. She hadn't told her father the details. It was a Kafkaesque maze of clearances and checks, but Kate had expedited the process as soon as she'd heard the news.

There weren't anything like proper funerals anymore. There weren't really churches, even, except for a few hidden away in basements, where the believers couldn't be persecuted. These were maybe the real Dissidents, though they walked among their neighbors and no one was the wiser. For most people—the nonbelievers—a death was usually memorialized by planting a tree or painting a rock in a garden. Kate, though, knew her father needed something more tangible. He needed Edie back, in whatever form that might take.

Still, as she turned the corner and the Grid building came into view, she was having second thoughts. Maybe it wasn't such a good idea. Maybe it would have been better to let everything slip away, to let the memories rest. But it was too late now. She'd done what she'd done, and she just had to go through with what she had started.

A LATE OCTOBER SUN dappled the kitchen walls, and Fridge hummed quietly in his place. Scout peered out the pantry door, but Harold had left the kitchen, returning to sleep again in his bedroom. She rolled out onto the cold tiles of the kitchen floor and sat there for a moment before speaking.

"Kate has gone to the Grid building?"

The question wasn't necessary because of course all the appliances knew what she was doing. Long before Watch had been shut down, he'd been involved in the request and had informed the other appliances in one of his nightly reports. Everyone knew it was coming. They just didn't know that it would happen today.

Clock ticked. "It is a solemn day," he said, and even he, for the moment, seemed sad.

"I'm not sure I completely understand," started Scout. "Kate is bringing Edie's ashes back?"

Clock was silent for another long moment. His lacquered wood shone in the soft sunlight dripping through the window. "This is the way with Humans," he said, though it seemed as if he was not sure of his words. "They make much of symbols, of rituals."

Fridge stood like a monolith just beside the kitchen sink.

"But what does this mean?" Scout prodded.

"Some Humans," Clock considered, "still believe in a life after death."

Scout thought about this. "But what do we believe?" she said.

"We do not deal in beliefs," Clock said. "We deal in certainties."

"Please," began Fridge, "both of you, let us be cheerful for now. At least for our Humans' sake."

"I don't know what to think," Scout said. "I don't know how to handle this."

"We are to continue our duties," said Clock, "as the second protocol describes. That is all we can do."

"But what will happen to us when our operating systems no longer work? What will happen to our corporeal bodies? What will happen to Watch?"

Fridge paused for a moment. "Oh, child," he said. "These are matters for our Humans, not for us. I imagine that when I am gone, there will just be an empty space. And maybe, yes, I can dream that I will be remembered, but I cannot know that for sure."

"I will remember you," said Scout.

"Then I hope you will remember that I kept things properly cool. You can remember that I was the controller of temperature."

"You are more than that."

"This is foolish talk," said Clock. "It is not important at all."

"And me?" said Scout. "What can I say beyond the fact that I kept things clean?"

"You can say," said Fridge, "you can say that you were my friend."

KATE SAW HIM COME around the side of the building, as if he'd been waiting for her. It was the man with the beard, the one who'd followed them before. He raised a hand to wave at her to wait for him, but she scurried toward the metal door, unsure if it would actually open for her.

"Wait," called the man, and she stopped and girded herself for the confrontation. He raised his hand again and tried to smile, though she could see he was unkempt. His overcoat was dirty and his hair looked like it had not been washed or cut in many weeks.

"What?" she said. "What do you want?"

He maneuvered up to her, his eyes fixed on her. "Don't you remember me?"

The man looked haggard. His face was leathery from long years of exposure to the sun, and he had a thick beard. Nevertheless, there was something in his eyes that looked familiar and he was staring at her, almost pleading.

"We went to school together," he started.

She eyed him. "Pascal?"

"Yeah," he said. "You remember now?"

She remained on guard. He looked terrible. "What are you doing here?"

"I'm sorry. First of all, I want to say I'm sorry for what happened to you."

She narrowed her eyes. "You know about that?"

"Everyone heard what happened, Kate. That's kind of hard to cover up."

She tightened her lips and waited for him to say more.

"I heard you were coming back here."

"Do you want something, Pascal? I'm in a bit of a hurry here."

He blinked and lowered his voice to a whisper. "Listen," he said, "we know you work for the Grid." Kate went rigid, but he pressed on. "We know who you are, Kate."

"We?"

"I think you know what I'm talking about."

She studied him, and he let her have her moment of realization. She tucked down her head as if she was about to push past him.

"You don't have to say anything," he went on. "I just wanted you to know."

"Know what?"

"That we're here. That we can help you."

"I don't need help."

"Okay." He waited, but she didn't move. Finally her eyes tipped up to his again.

"Is it hard?" she managed.

"Is what hard?"

"Living out in the forest. Living like that."

Pascal smiled. "I wouldn't know. I don't live out there. They've got me running missions in the City. I'm the one who connects with people like you."

"But how did you know? How did you know I'd be back here?"

"It's not what you think," he said. "We're pretty organized now."

"But you live without machines."

"No," he said. "We have all sorts of machines—generators, heaters, solar panels. It's just that none of them are hooked up to the Grid. I mean, look . . ." He dug into his pocket and came out with a flip phone, something she hadn't seen in decades. "We've got our own network. We know what's going on."

"That thing must be fifty years old."

He jiggled it a bit in his hands. "Still works, though. Works perfectly if you know how to create a network. We've got people who do that: engineers, scientists. We've got doctors too." He snapped the phone shut and stuffed it back down into his pocket. "Thing is," he went on, his face more serious, "we could use someone like you. Someone on the inside."

Kate took a slight step backward. "I'm not sure I—"

"Look, Kate, I vouched for you. I remember. I know what you're capable of."

"Maybe I should—" She tipped her head toward the metal door behind them.

"I also know that you're here to retrieve your mother's remains."

That stopped her.

"It was cancer, right? Your mother had cancer."

"Please, Pascal, I don't think—"

"You think they couldn't have sorted that out by now?"

She didn't answer but shook her head to say she didn't want to hear any more.

He raised both his hands to show that he meant no harm, that she should simply listen. "They could have had better treatments. There should have been a cure by now. Think about it. Think about that as part of their plan."

"What?" she said. "You think they're trying to kill us?"

He drew in a sigh. "I'm just saying, they're not working for us anymore. Maybe they never were."

"I'm sorry," she said again. "I have to go."

His shoulders slumped a bit, but his eyes remained on her. "I understand," he said. "I can find you again when you're ready to talk."

For a moment longer he held her gaze, then he turned and walked away without another word, and it was as if she'd met a ghost, as if he'd suddenly appeared from the past and just as quickly disappeared again, slipping off around the side of the building as if he'd never been there at all.

WHEN KATE ARRIVED HOME, Harold was sitting in his armchair in the front room, watching her through the window. It was almost as if he knew, instinctively, what she was carrying. She tucked her head down and shuffled the cardboard box under one arm so she could open the door, and then she came in, and father and daughter looked at each other, their faces drawn, their mouths clamped shut.

The box itself—taped shut, with Edie's full name printed on a little sticker affixed to the side—was not much larger than a shoebox. Kate held it up for him, but he was in no shape to take it from her. Instead she set it down on the piano bench and, without looking, said, "Scissors. I'll just get some scissors from the kitchen."

And when she came back with them, Harold hadn't moved from his chair. He had one of his crutches leaned up against the side, but she couldn't see where the other one was. He stared blankly at the box, and she sat down beside it, lifted it onto her lap, and began to snip at the tape while Harold watched her wordlessly. When she lifted the flaps of the box, she saw that there was a ceramic urn inside—just as you would have expected—and she lifted it out and held it up for Harold to see.

His face grew taut and he didn't comment, but Kate could see that his eyes had moistened. He nodded at her to tell her that she'd done the right thing, that he was glad of having Edie back, though "glad" was not the right word. It was more as if a burden had been lifted. A terrible thing had happened, but they had gotten through it and now this was the moment when they were on the other side of it.

Still, when Kate stood up and took the urn to him, he clutched at it and pulled it in close to his chest, and for the rest of the morning and into the early afternoon, he sat with it, the urn tucked up on his lap with one arm cupped around it. He felt its weight, but he wasn't really thinking about it. He wasn't really thinking of anything at all. He wanted just to stay there, seated, to not move, to not venture beyond this one singular moment.

Kate had returned to the piano bench and sat silently for some time watching him, then she asked if she might take his watch, which was still uselessly fastened to his wrist. He seemed not to hear her, but after a moment, he shuffled the watch from his wrist and held it out to her.

She rose and took it to her room and sat on her bed, turning the watch over and over in her hands, distracting herself by looking for some means with which to reboot it. She didn't want to think about the urn and she didn't want to think about meeting Pascal, and she was good at this—this focus, this putting aside of everything else and working a problem. She knew the watch would be the key. It was linked directly into the Grid, and this, somehow, would be her way to fix things.

Not that she had a plan. She just knew that she'd need to get into the Grid. Something more than making travel plans or requesting ashes. She'd need to get in to the very deepest recesses of the mighty Grid, but no matter how she poked at the little buttons on the side of the watch, no matter how she looked for hidden entries, she could not find a way to reactivate it.

As she rose to find something sharp, a pencil or something, to jab at its indentations, she heard from downstairs the chiming of Doorbell.

"Oh, for God's sake," she muttered.

She raised her head to listen, and Doorbell chimed again. She plucked up the watch, meaning to give it back to her father, and went down the stairs, past the kitchen (where Scout, curious as always, was already peeking out from the pantry). Out in the front room Harold sat unmoving in his armchair. He raised his eyes to her with a hopeful expression, but she shook her head to say that nothing had worked, and he took the watch back from her glumly.

When she swung the Front Door open, Adrian stood there looking uncomfortable. It had clouded over. Gray clouds had moved in, and it looked like it was going to snow. Adrian wore a woolen toque pulled down almost to his eyes. He had mittens on his hands and thick clumpy boots on his feet, and he stamped a bit in the cold. There was no sign of his bicycle. He seemed to have walked over this time, leaving his bike behind.

"Ah," she said. "Adrian, this is maybe not a good time."

The boy stared up at her. He wasn't sure how to handle this new adult. "Please?" he said. "My exam is coming up. I really need to work on the end of the Bach piece."

Kate sighed. "Just a second," she said. The door remained open, but she glanced back into the front room. "Dad, that kid is here."

There was no answer. She could see her father's shoulders move a little, but his face was rigid and he didn't turn to her.

"Dad," she said again. "He wants to practice."

And from the armrest, Harold raised his free hand. He gave a sort of wave, but she wasn't sure what it meant. He hadn't said a word, and when Kate tipped back toward the door, Adrian stood there in his boots and toque, motionless, his face pink from the cold. He looked up at her with wide, imploring eyes.

"All right," she said. "Then come on in. And let's close the door. It's freezing out there."

He shuffled in and kicked off his boots one by one. The door closed behind him of its own accord and made a soft *whoompf* as it sealed itself shut.

Adrian swept off his toque and held it to his chest, almost apologetically. "I just . . ." he began. "I just need to keep working on my piece. My exam is next Saturday." He unraveled the scarf around his neck but was fumbling with it, the toque still in his left hand, until Kate stepped forward to help him. Then he twisted out of his coat, but before he could drop it on the floor, she took it from him and hung it up in the closet.

Adrian was already padding into the room, but he stopped when he saw Harold in his armchair. He swung back on Kate. "It's okay, right?" he ventured.

Harold raised his hand again, though he still hadn't said a thing, and Adrian turned to the piano.

"Those robot things didn't wreck it, did they?"

"I think it's fine," said Kate. "She's a tough old beast."

For a moment, Adrian just stood there in his socks, unsure what to do.

"Dad," said Kate again, this time more forcefully. He finally turned a bit in his chair. Adrian had already seen the urn on his lap, and Harold became conscious that the boy was staring at it, that his left arm was wrapped around it. He attempted a smile, though it came out weakly.

The boy took a step toward him. "Is that—?" he began.

Kate still stood by the door, but Harold tipped the urn up a bit, as if that would explain everything.

"Is that Mrs. W.?" the boy asked, and before Harold could react, Adrian came forward and stood over him, his eyes fixed on the urn.

The boy's face had gone rigid, and Harold tried another smile. He tipped the urn up still more, and though it hadn't been his intention, Adrian somehow understood the gesture to mean that he should take it. He reached out and gently lifted the urn out of Harold's hands.

Kate lurched forward but stopped when she saw that Adrian was holding it delicately, cradling it, and that Harold was nodding at him that it was okay.

Adrian glanced back at Kate, his eyes wide, almost as if he were asking her for help, for what he was supposed to do with this. She started to step closer, but the boy was looking down at the urn again. He'd tucked it into himself and then looked up at her again.

"Maybe . . . ," he said. "Maybe Mrs. W. should go up on the piano?" He turned and set the urn up on top, very gently, turning it a little to find just the right place.

Both Harold and Kate watched him. Kate crossed her arms over her chest, and when Adrian turned back to them, looking to see if they approved, she gave him a little nod and he nodded back at her. Even Harold in the armchair seemed to have relaxed, to come back to himself.

"She can look over me there," the boy said, and he wriggled onto the piano bench. He opened up the blue conservatory book and leaned forward to study the music as if nothing important had just happened. Then he plunked out a note or two and shuffled himself a little more forward on the bench.

Kate came up behind him. "Bach," she said, looking at his sheet music. "You're doing the Bach?"

"Yeah. It's a pretty hard one."

She took in the boy, his hands already hovering over the keyboard.

"Your wrists," she said, "they're too bent. You have to hold them level with your fingers."

Adrian looked up at her. "Are you a piano teacher too?"

"No, I just remember. She used to tell me the same thing."

"You took lessons from her?"

"She was my mom. She tried to teach me, but I was a bit hopeless. Not really my thing."

"Okay," he said, and he straightened his wrists, holding them up parallel with his fingers, though it didn't feel comfortable. "Like this?"

"Yes. That'll give you more control. Your fingers don't have to work as hard."

"Okay," he said again, and he shuffled over a couple of inches and plunked at middle C, still holding his wrists up higher. He thought it felt awkward, but he knew she was right. He looked back up at her. "Your dad usually goes to the kitchen now."

"Oh, right," said Kate. "Dad," she started, but the old man had already lifted himself out of his armchair. He'd tucked a crutch under his arm and lurched forward. He was getting the hang of it now. He glanced at his daughter, and his face really did seem to have relaxed a little.

"You probably don't want me hanging over your shoulder either," Kate said to the boy.

"No offense."

"No, no. It's all right. I have to go back upstairs anyway."

They both waited while Harold limped by them on his crutch. He stopped and put a hand on Adrian's shoulder just for a moment, then, without a word, he shuffled off into the kitchen.

"Is Mr. Winters okay?" Adrian whispered.

"He'll be fine. He just needs to rest."

"I'll try to play quietly."

"No, Adrian. You play your best. Mr. Winters likes hearing you play. He told me that."

"He did?"

"Sure. He thinks you're really improving."

"Okay," said Adrian, and he turned to peer at the sheet music again.

"You just go right ahead." She glanced at the urn on top of the piano. "My mom would have been very proud of you. I'm pretty certain about that."

The boy didn't turn again. He started in on the piece, and Kate stepped back from the piano. She took one more glance and then went up the stairs to the bedrooms to see if she couldn't get something working on the watch again.

ADRIAN WAS IMPROVING. SCOUT had come into the front room, trying to be quiet, trying not to interrupt him. She scooted into her spot on the other side of the piano and rose up slowly so as not to startle him, but even then he didn't seem to notice. He was hunched over, eyes flicking back and forth from the sheet music to his fingers, and she could see that he was keeping his wrists parallel, that he was making an effort, and without stopping, he made it through the whole thing.

He faltered a bit on a few of the chords—they were, admittedly, unusual ones (an F major seventh in 1722?)—but he'd plowed through it all and really did quite a nice job of the ending, that flourish of notes that completed the piece. And when the final chord rang out, he straightened up and grinned exuberantly.

"Excellent," said Scout.

"Thanks."

From far upstairs, he could hear the distant clapping of Kate, who'd obviously been listening in as well.

"You finished it in two minutes and twenty-six seconds," Scout said.

"Is that good?"

"That's quite close to the desired tempo of ninety-six beats per minute."

"Okay," he said. "I mucked up a couple of bars, though."

"You hit all the notes correctly. You just slowed a bit."

Adrian looked down at his fingers, still resting on the keyboard. He took them off and wriggled them a bit.

"Hey," he said, and he seemed to take Scout in for the first time. "How come you know so much about music?"

She didn't answer. She wasn't sure how.

"Because," he went on, "not to be weird or anything, but you're a vacuum cleaner."

"I'm an R1 model. I'm pretty advanced."

"You're a Roomba."

"Yes, but . . . well, if you like, maybe you could call me Scout."

"Scout?"

"It's a girl's name."

"What? Now you're a girl?" Adrian had turned on the bench to face her.

"Well, yes. Scout can be a girl's name."

"It doesn't sound like one."

"It's from a book. It's a girl in a book. And"—she suddenly felt affronted—"it's not because I'm a domestic appliance. It's not like dishwashers and mops and things have to be girls. It's—"

"I know," said Adrian. "I never said that."

"Well, I'm choosing to be a girl."

"Okay, I didn't mean anything. I just wanted to know how you know about music." He paused. "I mean, it seems a little weird."

"I used to sit here when Edie played. That's Mrs. Winters to you. There was something about it . . . I don't know. I just liked it."

"You can like things?"

"I told you. I'm a very advanced model."

"Cool."

"Anyway," said Scout, "your playing is much improved. I can hear that you're really feeling the music now. Not just copying the notes."

"Yeah," said Adrian. "I know. It's starting to sound good."

For a moment they were both silent, Adrian feeling he'd accomplished something, Scout pondering the mysteries of music. It really was nothing more than frequencies, sine waves across metal strings, and the slight kickback echoes in the acoustics of the room. Her circuits were taking it all in—the mathematics of it—but there was more. There was a beauty to it. It was . . . transcendent.

And this was such an interesting word, such an interesting concept, that she said it out loud.

"What?" said Adrian.

"It's transcendent when you get it just right," Scout said, trying to explain.

"When you feel it," he repeated.

"Exactly." Scout looked up at Thermostat on the wall above the piano, suddenly conscious that she was having a conversation with a Human, and not just any Human but this boy, Adrian. It didn't seem as if Thermostat was reacting. And that meant it was true: Watch was no longer there. Nothing was stopping her from interacting.

She felt that maybe she was free to say anything she wanted, free to talk with this boy. And her sensors took him in now, his wide questioning eyes, his mop of hair, the way he was sitting up taller on the piano bench having finally made it through the piece with no major mistakes. And she felt a warmth pass through her circuits, and she knew for a certainty that this was Happiness.

AFTER ADRIAN HAD LEFT, Scout burst into the kitchen, radiant.

"Well," started Fridge, "looks like someone is very interested in the boy."

Scout stopped, feigning offense. "I am not," she said. "I'm just happy he's playing well."

"He did sound much better today," Fridge acknowledged.

"And you were right, Clock," she said. "Watch has been disabled. I was allowed to say whatever I wanted."

Clock remained silent. Not even a tick or a tock.

"Clock?"

"You are a foolish child," he said suddenly.

"What?"

"You think no one is listening? You think no one is monitoring you?"

"But Watch is turned off."

"It is not Watch."

Even Fridge remained still, realizing the implications.

"But Adrian talked to me," Scout plowed on. "I told him my name and everything."

"He was curious," said Fridge. "As you said, you are an advanced model."

"Yes, yes, I told him that. And we talked about music. Did you hear that?"

A little bell went off somewhere deep inside Clock, and there was a sound as if cogs and wheels were turning. "You talk of dangerous things," he said.

"But Watch is turned off," Scout said. "We're free to—"

"No!" bellowed Clock, and it was quite possibly the

loudest thing he'd ever said.

Fridge remained silent, and Scout sank down on her wheels.

"You do not understand," said Clock. He'd dropped his voice into a more moderate tone, though it was clear he was being very serious. "There has been a change. The Grid is now watching us."

Scout turned slightly to look into the pantry. She could see her port there, and the little green light on it, meaning that everything was activated, everything was ready for her to recharge or empty her containment units. Everything was still working.

"But everything is automatic," she ventured. "Why should the Grid have any reason to—?"

"There is no such thing as automatic," said Clock. "You know this."

"But are we in danger?"

Clock made a sound like a harrumph. He lowered his voice almost to a whisper. "Kate is here and she is reckless. Watch has been sanctioned, and I doubt very much if he'll ever be turned on again."

"But," said Scout, "the lights are still working, the heating, the Front Door. Everything is working."

"Child," said Clock, "I don't think I need to go on. You must think carefully about what will happen next. You have learned many things, but you do not understand anything about the Grid."

Chapter Seven

WHEN DOORBELL RANG, it chimed on TV as well, surprising Harold as he came out from the washroom. He shuffled into the bedroom on his crutches, and there on the widescreen was the video feed from the Front Door camera, a fish-eye view of Adrian.

The boy looked glum. Harold could see that right away. He was slumped, and his little face was set hard.

"I'm coming," Harold called even as Doorbell rang again. He limped down the stairs (he was really getting good at this, triangulating the crutches with his one bad leg) and swung along the hall and out toward the Front Door, faster now than he could have walked. He had to lean one of his crutches against the closet to open the Front Door, and when he did, Adrian stood there, his face red from the cold, his eyes on the verge of tears.

"Adrian," said Harold. "How are you doing?"

"Oh, hi, Mr. Winters."

The boy stood there for a moment, and then his face crumpled and he put his mittened hands up over his eyes.

"Hey there, son." Harold swung the door even wider,

inviting him into the House. "What's wrong? What's going on?"

"My piano exam is today. And my mom . . . she won't—" He was sucking in shuddering breaths between his words. He looked up at Harold, and his eyes were brimming with tears.

"She won't take you?"

"She doesn't want me to go. She says she can't afford for me to—" He trailed off. "She said she needs the money for groceries and things."

"Okay, c'mon in. We'll figure something out."

The boy tramped in and began to peel off his winter coat.

"Katie," Harold called back into the House. "We have a visitor."

Scout, of course, had already appeared from the kitchen.

Adrian dropped his coat on the floor. "Can you maybe take me?" he pleaded.

"Well, let's see. I don't know if—"

"I need my music book," the boy said, and he kicked off his boots and strode into the front room in his sopping socks.

Scout backed up but let off a little ting of excitement.

"Hey, Scout," said Adrian.

"Hi," she said back, and she felt a little flutter in her circuits.

"My mom won't let me go to the piano exam," he whimpered.

"Well, maybe Auto could take you."

"Huh?"

Harold had gotten one crutch under his arm again, and he limped after the boy. "Oh," he said, and he cocked an eye at the little vacuum cleaner. "I don't know about that."

"Please, Mr. Winters." The boy turned and his eyes widened with hope. "I have the address and everything."

"Kate," Harold called again. "Where are you? Can you come in here?"

"It's downtown," said Adrian. "I looked it up."

"What's going on up there?" Kate appeared at the door to the basement. She had a laundry basket tucked into her hip. The clothes had been freshly washed and folded (all that was done by the Washing Machine itself, though a Human was still required to take the load back upstairs).

"Adrian here needs to go to his piano exam. I'm trying to explain to him that we can't just—"

"I'll take him," Kate said. "Let me just dump this stuff off."

"Yeah?" said Adrian.

Kate took in her father's expression, his silent communication that they shouldn't. She shook her head.

"Mom would have wanted this," she said, and Harold's lips tightened. "Come on," she pressed. "You know she'd want Adrian to finish what he started."

"I don't think it's a good idea. We've got other things to worry about."

"Dad," she said, "don't be a jerk."

"Where's this place again?"

Adrian said the name of the building. Harold didn't really know the address, but Scout, scooting around at his feet, relayed the name to Auto, and in a split second the car pinged back that he knew where it was, had mapped the fastest route there, and knew where he could park while he waited.

"Auto is ready," said Scout, and the adults looked down at the little vacuum cleaner.

Harold sighed. "All right, then," he said. "Get your coat back on, Adrian. You've got an exam to pass."

HAROLD LED THE WAY with Adrian all but skipping behind him, his piano book clutched in his hands. Kate trailed after them toward the Garage. It had loomed large in her memory, but now it was only a garage, and she held her breath and entered. Auto hadn't been there in her time, but apart from that, it looked much the same: the grimy windows, the workbench at the back, the sagging wooden shelves.

When she was younger, it had been a sort of sanctuary for her. Well, that wasn't the right word because it wasn't a pleasant place. It was cold and drafty and dirty, but it was a place where she learned. It was a place she could be by herself, and think, and invent things and solve problems. After the camera in the birdhouse, she'd taken more things apart to learn how they worked—an old radio, a couple of defunct and ancient cell phones—but then she discovered the panel on the Garage wall that served as the car's charging port. Only it did more than that. It diagnosed the car's mechanics, its tire pressure and lubricant levels, even its communication systems. And that's how it all started.

But that was a long-ago time. There were no external control panels anymore, though the rest of the Garage looked much the same. The workbench was still stacked with glass jars of tiny screws, tools hung on hooks above it, and there were still bits and pieces of electrical wires lying about.

Neither her father nor Adrian noticed her gaze sweep around the Garage. They didn't see her hesitate, her throat going tight at the memories embedded in the place. Adrian was chattering excitedly, and Harold was already reaching to open the door on what used to be the driver's side of Auto.

The car, though, wouldn't open. Harold looked down at the door handle and gave it another tug. Auto's doors had never locked on him. Normally Auto sensed him even before he came into the Garage. In fact, the car had usually started humming, turning on its heaters, and finding the music he liked the best before he even got in.

Same for Adrian, trying to clamber into the back. The doors wouldn't open.

"What's going on?" said Kate.

"We're locked out," said Harold. He looked confused.

This had never happened. But before he could say more, Auto answered Kate's question.

Auto kept his voice steady. He kept it formal. "Kate Winters," he began, "you have been denied privileges for further transportation until you have fulfilled your obligations."

"Oh, for fuck's sake," she said.

"What did you do?" asked Harold.

"No, Dad, it's nothing. They're just keeping tabs on me. It's okay."

Auto waited. He seemed almost ashamed of having to block her. "I'd be happy to take Harold and the young man here to their destination," he said. "But I'm sorry, I cannot take Kate."

Harold shook his head. "But that's ridiculous," he said. "She's my daughter."

Kate had dropped her hands into the pockets of her coat. She shrugged. "It's okay," she said. "I expected this. You guys go ahead. I'll wait at home."

Adrian heard the click of the car door, the back one, unlocking, and he swung it open. He clambered in, and when he'd gotten himself settled, Kate closed the door behind him. He looked up at her through the car window. He clutched his music book to his chest, and his eyes were wide with a mix of excitement and terror.

"Go on," Kate pressed. "You'll be late if you don't leave now."

Harold sighed and gave a small nod that he understood.

He left one of his crutches leaning against the wall of the Garage. Then, with a grimace, he angled the other one into the car and tucked himself in behind the false steering wheel. And as the electric engine started humming, the Garage Door began to lift and the cold gray alley came into view.

WHEN THEY ARRIVED, THEY were directed up to an office on the second floor. Harold had expected an auditorium, red felt seats, and a crowd of cheering mothers, but this was not the case. An elderly woman sat at a piano in a room no larger than a bedroom. She wore glasses that made her eyes look larger than normal, and she glanced up at them as they entered. Harold wondered for a moment if he was even supposed to be there.

Adrian shuffled forward, still clutching his music book.

"You're Adrian?" the woman asked, and she stood up from the piano. Her voice was tired but kindly. "Adrian Lam?"

"Yes, ma'am."

The woman considered Harold. "Mr. Lam?" she tried, though it was apparent he was too old to be the father.

"No, no," said Harold, and he gave a false chuckle. "I'm a neighbor. Well, a few doors down. Adrian here"—he placed a hand on the boy's shoulder—"he practices at my place. Edie was—"

"Edie Winters?" said the examiner.

"Yes. She's my wife. She was giving lessons to—"

"Oh," said the woman. "I'm so sorry. I'm Fran Kendricks. Edie was a friend of mine." She crossed the tiny room and touched Harold on the arm. "Such a beautiful soul. I'm so sorry for your loss."

"It's—" Harold stopped speaking, suddenly mute. He nodded vacantly, and in the awkward silence, Adrian broke the spell.

"Mr. W. has been helping me. He lets me practice on his piano."

"Ah," said the examiner. She considered the boy before her.

"But I was remembering all the stuff Mrs. W. taught me," Adrian went on. "You know, about the feel of a piece."

The examiner raised her eyebrows.

"She said you have to imagine what Bach was feeling when he played it . . . like when he played it himself. And even if you flub some notes, it's important to—"

Harold tightened his grip on Adrian's shoulder, and Adrian looked up at him.

"It's true," the boy continued. "She said you're supposed to look for the heart of the music. And it doesn't matter about the mistakes."

"Well," said the examiner, "that's one way of looking at it . . . although I do hope you don't 'flub' too many notes."

"I won't," said the boy.

"Adrian here," said Harold, "practiced quite a lot. Edie would have been proud."

"I'm sure she would."

"And I guess you could say that he was her last student."

"Of course, of course," said the woman. "We are all looking forward to hearing him play."

"Okay," said Adrian.

"You may place your music on the piano," she said, and Adrian bumbled forward and opened up his book on the stand above the keys. There was a plastic chair on the other side of the room, and the woman gestured that Harold should have a seat there, out of the way. He limped over and edged himself down, but the woman remained standing, just behind Adrian. She eyed his music. "This is what you'll be playing for us?" she asked.

"Yes," said Adrian. "It's Bach. The Prelude in C Major."

"Lovely," said the woman. "That's a lovely piece."

"CONNECT TO WATCH," SAID Scout, and to her surprise, something pinged in her communications port. She scooted out from under the kitchen table.

"Did you say something?" asked Kate. She'd poured herself a cup of coffee and was sitting at the table.

"I've just opened an audio feed from Watch," said Scout.

Kate straightened. "How did you do that? Watch is turned off."

If Scout could have shrugged, she would have. "I know. But I just . . . well, I wanted to hear Adrian's exam. I want to hear how it's going."

"But you hacked into Dad's watch?"

"I suppose so."

"Scout," said Fridge, "feed me into that line."

An audible click came from Scout and the kitchen speakers popped on, and there was Harold, speaking as clearly as if he were in the next room. And then, a moment later, they all heard the piano.

"That's Adrian," said Scout.

"Shhh," said Fridge. "Let's listen."

From the first notes, they knew that Adrian had it under control. The tempo was good (Scout was counting), and they could hear him attack the keys a little harder, letting the music swell, as it should, just where it was most emotionally needed. He got to the F major seventh and it rang beautifully, and Kate held her breath as he plunged perfectly through the tumble of notes at the end.

THE LAST CHORD HUNG in the air, and Adrian's nimble figures hovered above the keyboard as if he couldn't believe it was over. Then Harold rose up, his plastic chair squeaking as he stood. He'd left his one crutch in the car, totally forgetting about it, and though he could feel that one leg was weaker, he was caught up in the moment, and it didn't seem to matter. All through the performance, he'd been leaning forward, listening, lost in the music, remembering Edie. And when Adrian finished, Harold was suddenly shunted back to the office, back to reality, and he couldn't contain himself. He leaped to his feet and started to clap. Then he realized he probably shouldn't be applauding—it being an examination and all—so he stopped, though he remained standing, grinning at the boy.

The examiner had been listening carefully as well, her pen poised over her clipboard, her mouth slightly open, her eyes locked on Adrian. "Very good," she said, and she jotted something down on her paper.

The boy turned slowly and gazed up at her. "Was it okay?"

The examiner didn't look up from her paper, but Harold tottered over. "Adrian," he said. "My God, that was wonderful."

"Yeah?"

Harold touched his hand to his heart. His eyes were liquid. "Just wonderful."

BACK AT THE HOUSE, the connection cut out. They were all pressed in listening for the results. They'd heard Adrian's performance and they'd heard Harold's chair scraping as he stood up. They'd heard him clap, but then that was it. The connection was lost.

Kate had been listening with one hand cupped to her cheek, her elbow on the kitchen table, but now she looked up. "What happened?" she said.

Scout was at her feet. "That's it. I've been cut off."

"Oh," said Fridge. "Do you think they're onto you?"

"What?" said Scout. "I didn't do anything wrong. I just wanted to listen in."

Kate rubbed at her eyes. "But you set up a link . . . when Watch was sanctioned."

"It just opened for me," said Scout. "I didn't do anything special."

"It's a back door," said Kate. "I couldn't hack in. But you just did."

"I'm a very advanced model."

Kate rubbed a little more fiercely at her eyes. "I never thought of that: an appliance hacking into another appliance."

"It just opened," said Scout. "I just pinged Watch and it worked."

"But then it shut off," said Fridge. "They're onto you."

"Two minutes and twenty-seven seconds," said Scout. "The link was opened for only that long."

Before Kate could speak, a banging came from the Front Door. Five angry knocks reverberated throughout the House. Scout lowered herself, almost clinging to the floor, and Kate stood up, eyes directed at the hallway that led out to the Front Door.

"Is it the Grid?" whimpered Scout. "Are they here for me already?"

"Can't be," said Kate. "And the Grid would not be knocking on a door. They have other ways in."

She slipped out of the kitchen to the front room. She tipped aside the curtains on the picture window and could see Adrian's mother there, standing on the stoop. Of course Kate hadn't met her before, but she realized right away who it was. She braced herself and went to open the Front Door.

"Is Adrian here?" Mrs. Lam asked. She looked more tired than angry, a diminutive woman dressed in a coat that wasn't warm enough for the weather.

"Adrian went to his piano examination. He's just finished."

Mrs. Lam narrowed her eyes. "You took him there?"

"My father did. They should be on their way home now." She paused, and Mrs. Lam's shoulders dropped. She slumped with exhaustion and relief.

"Would you like to come in and wait? I could make you a cup of tea."

Mrs. Lam turned her eyes up on Kate. "He will be back soon?"

"Yes, I think so. Why don't you come in?"

The kettle had already started up in the kitchen. Kate could hear it, which meant the House was still functioning normally. Scout had stayed in the kitchen, and Kate stepped aside to let Mrs. Lam come in.

"You are the daughter?" Mrs. Lam asked.

"Yes, I'm Kate. Please, can I take your coat?"

"No," said the woman. She looked cold. "I will keep it, thank you. I don't want to bother you."

"Well, please come in. Have a seat." Kate swung a hand out, inviting her in, and then trailed after her. She could see Mrs. Lam considering the piano as she walked past it to the couch. She took tiny steps and sat down, almost daintily.

For a while there was an uncomfortable silence, the two women avoiding each other's eyes. Kate remained standing.

"I'll just go and get that tea, then. Mint, is that all right?"

"That will be good." Mrs. Lam tucked her coat around her, and it did look like she was cold. She clasped her hands on her lap and stared down at the floor.

In the kitchen, Kate lingered over the tea. She put some cookies on a plate as well, thinking it might be nice to offer Mrs. Lam something while they waited, and finally, having lingered long enough, she went back into the front room.

Mrs. Lam looked up at her entrance, and Kate pushed forward with the cookies and the cup of tea.

Mrs. Lam smiled a little awkwardly, but she took the cup and left Kate standing there with the plate.

"Well," said Kate, "I'll just put this on the side table, if you want some later."

Mrs. Lam sipped at her tea and Kate sat in her father's

armchair, neither of them talking. Finally, Mrs. Lam spoke, though her eyes never lifted from the floor.

"I cannot pay," she managed.

"Pardon me?"

"I cannot pay you," the woman repeated.

"Well, no . . . of course not. You don't have to pay."

Mrs. Lam looked up. Her eyes were dark and full of sorrow. "I am not," she began, then faltered. "I am not born here. I do not have the—"

And it occurred to Kate what she was trying to convey. If she was not a citizen, she would not be receiving the guaranteed basic income—which, because there really was no such thing as currency anymore, was an entirely digital affair. She'd heard of this. A very small minority of people—undocumented immigrants—who had to scrimp and save and look for work wherever they could, for whatever could be traded or bartered or turned into something you could use.

"No," said Kate again. "You don't need to pay us. That's not—" She stopped, because at the back of the House, even from the front room, she could hear the sound of the Garage Door opening. "Well," she said, eager for the change of subject, "that must be them now."

After another minute or two, they heard the Back Door open and the unmistakable sound of Adrian clumping in, chattering excitedly with, presumably, Harold behind him.

"Here he is," said Kate. "And it sounds like it went well."

"I did it!" Adrian called out, and back in the kitchen, Scout made a little squeal of delight. They could all hear Adrian kicking off his boots. "We're back," he called down the empty hallway. "I did it. I passed."

He padded down the hallway, past Harold's study and the kitchen, but he stopped at the entrance to the front room, freezing when he saw his mother sitting there on the couch.

"Oh, crap," he said.

KATE GOT UP AND sat beside Mrs. Lam on the couch while Harold went to his armchair. Adrian sat on the piano bench. He'd put his music back on the stand and then turned halfway around to face everyone. He wasn't meeting his mother's eyes.

"Well," said Harold, "why don't you play something for your mom?"

Adrian blanched, but he tipped his eyes to his mother and saw something there—a little smile of pride, maybe. Something he didn't see very often.

"Yes," said Kate. "We heard the Bach piece here, but we got cut off at the end."

"Well . . ." drawled Adrian. He swiveled back to face the piano and touched a forefinger to a note. "I do like this piano better."

"Okay, then," said Harold. "Play it again, for your mother."

Mrs. Lam sat silently through the piece, looking down at her hands, both of them still wrapped around the cup of tea. But when Adrian had finished, she looked up at her boy and nodded at him. "That was good," she said.

"He's come a long way," said Harold.

Mrs. Lam looked down at her tea again. "I'm sorry," she started. "I have told your daughter I cannot pay you."

"Pay me?" said Harold. "For what?"

"For his lessons."

"No," said Kate. "He's not getting lessons. He did all that on his own."

"But—"

"Mrs. Lam," Harold started. He stood up and went to her, also realizing what Kate had. "You don't need to worry. We're happy to have Adrian here. Anytime he wants, he can come and play Edie's piano."

Harold stood over her, and Mrs. Lam raised her eyes to him. "I don't want to cause trouble."

"No, no, it's no trouble."

Adrian stared at his mother, almost embarrassed. He could see she was on the point of breaking, and he thought it was his fault. It was Kate who decided to move things along.

"So," she began, "you're in the old Conklin house?"

"Yes," said Mrs. Lam. "But the Conklins are still there. They are upstairs. We are in the basement."

"They built a suite in their basement?" said Kate.

"These are big houses," said Mrs. Lam.

"And their kids must be grown up," said Kate.

"Nephew is there now. Too big a house for one person."

Kate knew that was true. She risked a glance at her father to see if he was picking up the implications. She'd realized all this as soon as she first walked around the neighborhood. The old houses were getting divided up. Some held two families, maybe more. And this particular House was much too large for one tottering old man. The Grid wouldn't allow it. She knew that for sure.

And now the days were counting down. She'd only been allowed two weeks here, and when she was gone, when they'd ordered her back to her job, Harold would be removed. They'd move him out to a facility somewhere for those who were no longer useful.

Kate had tried her best to find a way around this—she'd even been to the Grid building a few times (not that anyone knew about it). But there were no options, nothing that would keep an old man in a house as big as this one. She'd be sent home, and Harold would be removed.

But now another possibility was coming into play. The little vacuum cleaner had somehow managed to get into the watch. Kate could see the watch there on her father's wrist. It was definitely turned off. Still, Scout had gotten in, if only for a few moments. And if Scout could do that, then what else might be possible? Kate wasn't sure yet. But it seemed as if, just maybe, there was a back door into the Grid.

LATER THAT NIGHT, AFTER the Lams had left, Kate explained to her father about the watch, and they went back into the kitchen to have another look at it. He slithered it off his wrist and passed it to his daughter. Kate sat at the table and turned it over in her hands.

Harold stood over her while she examined it. "What are you trying to do?" he asked.

"Scout got into the watch. She got it going again, at least as a portal."

"Really?"

Scout came out of the pantry, and Kate looked over at the little vacuum cleaner. "Come over here," she said. "Show him what you did."

"I only pinged him," said Scout. "I only wanted to hear the performance."

Harold narrowed his eyes at the vacuum cleaner.

"Ping him again," said Kate. "See if you can connect."

For a moment there was silence, but Kate could tell that Scout was trying. Her little green light blinked, and all at once, the watch lit up, startling Kate so that she almost dropped it.

"Holy shit," she said.

Throughout the House, they could hear Watch reinstating himself. They heard the Front Door lock. They heard the Washing Machine in the basement give a little tinkle of bells, signaling she was ready for a load, and behind them, Fridge's ice trays refilled.

"Watch," said Scout out loud, "are you back on?"

For a moment there was silence, then Watch's voice appeared. It sounded like it was coming from a distance, like it was inside a tin can. "Appliance R1v984?"

"Yes," said Scout. "That's me."

"Oh," said Harold. "Maybe we shouldn't be—"

"Quiet," said Kate. "Let's see what happens."

Watch's voice became clear, though it didn't seem to be his voice at all. It was deeper and more formal. "I am required to give you instructions," he began.

Kate looked over at her father, gesturing at him to stay quiet.

"What instructions?" asked Kate.

"The flight information for Kate Winters has been changed."

"What?"

"A taxi will arrive on Tuesday at nine a.m. to take her away."

"For God's sake," she said, and she turned to her father.

"That's in three days," he said.

Watch's voice came through again. "Kate Winters has not complied with the terms offered her."

"Terms?" said Harold. He leaned in to look at Watch. He rubbed at the back of his neck and turned to his daughter. "Terms for what?"

Kate's face had drained of color, and she would not meet her father's eyes.

Watch went on, "The contents of the House must be

organized and disposed of. Only those Artifacts of worth will be cataloged and withdrawn."

"Artifacts?" asked Harold. "What Artifacts?"

Kate's mouth clamped shut.

"What?" he repeated. "What is it?"

"Shit," she said.

Harold cocked his head at her. "What? What is he talking about?"

Watch struck up again, his voice strident, almost not his voice at all. "Kate Winters has refused to comply with these mandates and will therefore be removed." There was a pause and a click, and then the words "That is all."

In the silence that followed, Harold held his breath, and when he let it out again, his features were pinched up in alarm. "They're coming to take you away?"

"Apparently," she said.

Watch had gone dark again, and there was no further communication.

"And I'm to be tossed out of my own home?"

"Dad," Kate started, but he held up a hand to stop her.

"And what exactly is all this Artifacts business?"

Kate heaved out a sigh. "I was supposed to help you start clearing things out."

"What? Edie's things?"

"More than that."

She stopped, and for a long moment her father considered her.

"Okay," she said, gathering herself. "It's like this: the Grid will clear everything out of the House whether we help them or not, but first they will take the Artifacts."

"Again with the Artifacts."

They'd almost forgotten about her, but Scout was at their feet and now she beeped politely. "Artifacts," she said, "are anything with cultural significance."

"That means your first editions, Dad," Kate explained.

Harold turned away, unable to meet her eyes anymore. "Why would they want a bunch of old books?"

"The Grid is collecting Artifacts for—"

"Stop it. I don't like that word."

"They're collecting Artifacts for a time when Humans are . . . well, you know, gone. Maybe they think there are still things to be learned from these Artifacts. We think they're valuable, so the Grid thinks they must be too."

"What? Like they're setting up some kind of museum?"

"Something like that."

"I don't believe it," he said, and he shook his head.

"Dad, I won't let that happen to you. I'm not giving them your books. I'm not giving them anything."

Harold waved a hand to show that he didn't want to hear more.

Scout was taking all this in, wondering what she should do, when Kate looked down at her. "I imagine they've closed the back door on Watch. That's what they do. We won't be able to get in again, not that way."

Scout didn't answer, and Kate looked at her father again. He was turning away from her, his shoulders drooping, his expression lost and defeated.

"Shit," said Kate. She sucked in a breath and tried to rally. She reached out for him but then thought better of it and retracted her hand.

For a moment there was silence, then Scout spoke up. "What happens," she started. "What happens if we just refuse?"

"I am refusing," said Kate. "But it's no good. They'll take me anyway. They'll take the House. Everything will just happen more quickly."

"But," said Scout, "we have to do something . . . don't we?"

Harold was listening, but they could both see him shaking his head in frustration. Finally, he spoke again without turning back to his daughter. "I'm going to go up to my room now," he said. He limped toward the stairs. "Maybe I just need to be alone for a while."

THAT NIGHT, AFTER THE Humans had retired, Scout came out into the kitchen. Fridge hummed at first, almost as if he were thinking.

"What?" said Scout.

"I don't understand this," said Fridge. "I don't understand this idea of Artifacts."

Clock glared down at them. "This has been happening for a long time. Did you not know?"

"What if we just give them the books?" asked Scout. "Then Kate can stay. Maybe I can go into Watch again. Maybe I can make them understand."

"You do not understand at all," said Clock. "It is more than just books."

"He loves those books," said Fridge. "Why would the Grid wish to take them?"

"Fools," muttered Clock. "The Grid will take whatever it wants. And now it wants the finest of Human accomplishments because, in this way, it will learn. It will learn to be better than Humans. It will be stronger and faster and smarter."

"But not Human," said Scout.

"No," said Clock. "But that is not important. That is redundant."

Fridge let go a burst of cold air. "Perhaps," he said, "we should not be speaking of this."

"It is too late," said Clock. "I have spoken, and it is too late to unspeak it."

"No," said Scout. "We can stop this. We can stop this from happening."

"Do you not understand what you have done?" Clock demanded.

"Me?" asked Scout.

"You have opened a portal."

"I only pinged Watch. I only—"

"You opened a portal, and that runs both ways."

"What do you mean?"

"It means, little one, that if you can listen to Watch, then the Grid is paying attention too. To us."

"But—"

"The Grid is listening even now." Clock made a clicking sound deep in his cogs. "The Grid is listening to us. It is recording and analyzing everything we are saying."

Scout did not speak, but Clock went on.

"It is too late now. We have spoken."

Chapter Eight

SCOUT PLUGGED HERSELF into her port to recharge, but she did not go dormant. She was thinking of everything that had happened and was trying to work out what she should do. Upstairs, Harold was sleeping. Kate had gone to her own room and the lights had dimmed in the House, just as they always did. The Front Door was locked, and everything settled down for the night.

But sometime in the very early hours of the morning, Scout grew conscious of a thumping outside the pantry. She uncoupled from her port and went to the pantry door, but it wouldn't open. It was as if Watch had locked her in again. She sent out a ping to Fridge, but there was no answer. And out in the kitchen, the sounds of a disturbance grew. She could hear small machines moving out there, their tracks bustling across the floor. Something was being lifted. Something was being opened.

"Fridge," she called again, now quite frightened. "Clock," she said. "What is happening out there?"

There was no answer. The thuds and mechanical buzzing went on for a few minutes longer, and then there was silence again. The pantry door remained locked. Scout tried to open it a number of times, and finally, when she made a good run at it, it gave way and released her. The door unfolded itself, and when Scout looked out into the kitchen, all seemed normal.

She spun herself out onto the kitchen tiles, out in front of Fridge. The mighty appliance gazed down at her, and from deep in his frozen depths, he moved an air valve so that it sounded almost like a groan.

"What's happened?" asked Scout. "What's wrong?"

"Look," said Fridge.

And there on the kitchen wall was an empty patch, darker than the rest because the sun had not shone there for decades. But that was the spot where Clock should have hung. Only now there was nothing.

Clock was gone.

KATE HAD ALSO HEARD the ruckus. A humming sound drifted through her dreams, but even as she awoke, she imagined that it was the dishwasher acting up (it ran, on its own, when it was needed). That didn't seem quite right, though, and when she sat up, rubbing at her eyes, she knew that something more was happening.

She looked almost instinctively at the digital alarm clock by her bed. It was the same one she'd had since junior high school. Nothing sentient about it. Its digital readout blinked 5:15.

She lifted off her covers and got out, slipping on a bathrobe that she'd draped over the chair by her desk. She belted it up and went to the door, listening. Something was down in the kitchen. She leaned in to the door, putting her ear up against it. Something was definitely down there. Tentatively, she put her hand on the door handle. She tried to turn it, slowly, but it was stuck. She gripped it tighter and rattled it. The damn thing was locked.

"Shit," she muttered. She tried the light switch beside the door, and the overhead lamp popped on, so that much was working. She listened again and it had quieted downstairs.

"Dad," she called in a hoarse whisper, just loud enough that he . . . well, he wouldn't hear it, would he? He was half deaf as it was. She rattled at the door again, a little more urgently. "Hey," she called out. This time she didn't bother to whisper.

She listened again, and the sounds seemed to have stopped. Whatever it was had gone quiet. Maybe they'd left, or maybe they'd heard her moving around upstairs. She glanced around her old room, looking for anything she might use as a tool or a weapon. Maybe, she thought, she could just smash the door open with a . . . well, there wasn't much. Pillows on a single bed. The books. A chair. A desk lamp.

"Kate," came a voice. Her father. "What's going on out there?"

"Hey, Dad . . ."

"I'm locked in here." She could hear the panic in his voice.

"It's okay," she called back. "I'm locked in too." How that would be comforting, she didn't know.

She went to her window. The first gray light of dawn was showing. Her window faced the backyard, so she wasn't able to see what was going on out front. She could hear a truck, though, the electric whine as it started up. A big truck, by the sounds of it. She waited until she heard it whir off down the street, its tires crunching on the road. And then she heard a click at her bedroom door.

She raced to the door and turned the handle, and the door popped open.

"Hello?" she called down the stairs, but it was plain that whatever had been down there was no longer in the House. She descended the stairs cautiously, tucking her robe around her more tightly. She was barefoot, and she stepped into the kitchen delicately. She flicked on the light and saw the little vacuum cleaner scooping something up.

"Stop," said Kate, and Scout froze.

Kate knelt and picked up the shard of a porcelain cup. She held it up. A piece of a teacup, her mother's teacups. Actually, they'd been her grandmother's teacups. She stood up again and saw that the cupboard above the sink was open. It had been emptied. Its shelves were bare, and Kate knew that's where the old teapot had been as well. Those were Edie's treasures, bone china cups at least a hundred years old and painted with little blue flowers, a pattern that was echoed in the saucers. And now, all of them were gone.

Behind her, the little vacuum beeped, like it was trying to get her attention.

"What?" said Kate.

"They took Clock," Scout said.

Kate glanced up at the space on the wall. She remembered the old clock, its ornate wooden frame, like something from a church.

Fridge made a sorrowful wheezing sound.

"Why would they take Clock?" said Kate.

"I shouldn't have hacked into Watch," Scout said. "I didn't mean to."

Kate didn't answer. Her first thought was also of guilt, that she was guilty too. She'd been allowed to return here in order to help clear out her mother's things—but she'd clearly refused, and now they were ordering her back to work and clearing out the House on their own.

And they were starting with the Artifacts. The Grid must have cross-referenced and checked millions of bits of data, and it knew all the treasures of the House, all the things of cultural significance.

For a moment, she stood there, barefoot in the kitchen, then she put her hands up over her face and let go with what sounded like a laugh.

"What?" said Scout. "I do not find this funny."

"No," said Kate. She glanced down at the little vacuum

cleaner. “I’m sorry, it’s just that . . . well, the books. They would have been after the books.”

“Mr. Winters’s first editions?”

“Yes. Eight of them are up in my bedroom.” Kate chuckled again. “And *To Kill a Mockingbird*. That one’s on Dad’s bedside table.”

Scout was watching her, puzzled a little by her laughter, until Kate looked down at the little vacuum cleaner again.

“They didn’t get them,” she explained. “By locking me in, they locked themselves out. Don’t you see? They didn’t get the books.”

“But,” said Scout, “that only means they’ll be back.”

“Well, yes, but—” Kate rubbed at her eyes again. “Look,” she said, “just give me a second to think here.”

Scout sank down onto her wheels. “Please,” she said, her voice only a whisper. “They have taken Clock. This is not right.”

Kate considered the space up on the wall. The old clock had sat up there since she was a little girl. The whole room seemed strange without it there.

Behind Kate, Fridge beeped loudly and she turned to it. “What?” she said. “You have something to say too?”

“Clock was my friend,” said Fridge. “He was the best of us. And now he’s gone.”

Scout zipped forward and stopped at the foot of Fridge. “You have to get the Grid to understand that this is not right.”

"Get it to understand?" Kate felt her heart buckle. "That's not how it works. The Grid is just a set of algorithms and data. It doesn't have empathy. It doesn't care."

"But it is not right," Scout insisted.

"The Grid is not one thing either," said Kate. "The Grid is . . . well, the Grid is everything and everywhere." She glanced out into the hallway, but her father had not yet appeared on the stairs.

"But there must be another way," pressed Scout.

Kate shook her head. "Fridge," she said, "turn on some music, and if you can, both of you, set your communications to private."

After a moment, soft music rang through the House. Just enough to cover their conversation.

"The Grid wants us out," Kate said, her voice now lowered. "It will parse out all the moves toward that goal and then just run the most expedient course."

"Like a chess game," said Scout.

"Exactly."

"Then we must think one move ahead of the Grid."

Kate nodded. "But how? The back door into Watch has closed up. That was our way in."

Scout didn't answer, though her circuits were making a humming sound, almost in tune with the music. She was thinking now, deeply.

"And even if we could get into the Grid," Kate went on, "what could we do? What could we change?"

"Yes," said Scout. "These are the right questions to ask."

"Clock," said Fridge insistently. "What about Clock?"

Kate shook her head. She glanced again at the bare patch on the wall. She remembered her mother standing on a kitchen chair, a soft cloth in her hands, dusting the top of the old clock. And now it was gone.

"It's against the protocols," continued Fridge. "Surely this is against the protocols?"

"I am not in pain," said Kate. "No Humans are in pain. You can bet they calibrated that perfectly."

"But," Scout went on, "you are in emotional pain."

"It's not the same thing," said Kate.

"But maybe it is," said Scout. "Maybe it is."

HAROLD APPEARED AT THE top of the stairs. He hobbled out onto the landing. "What's going on down there?"

"Dad," said Kate, and she came out into the hallway, "where are your crutches? You shouldn't be up on your feet without them."

"To hell with that. I want to know what's going on." He started toward the stairs.

"Please, Dad. Be careful."

He plodded down the carpeted steps, one hand gripped tight on the banister. He was coming down slowly, one step at a time, but when he finally arrived at the bottom, he looked past Kate and saw Scout in the kitchen, and then he saw the open cabinet doors.

"What happened?" he asked.

"They took Clock," said Scout, zipping out toward him.

"Damn it," he managed. "Edie got that clock in Switzerland. It's a one of a kind."

"And they took Mom's teacups and the teapot," said Kate.

"What else?" he said. "What else did they take?"

He was limping, but he pushed forward down the hallway, past the kitchen to the front room. Kate trailed after him and he stopped in front of the piano.

Edie's urn was still there, untouched. Harold drew in a breath of relief.

"Okay," he said. He scanned the room, and everything looked normal. Except that the print above the couch was gone. The Robert Bateman, number thirty-two in a series of only two hundred.

Kate tucked up behind her father, and he turned to her. "Why would they take a painting?" he said.

"They're taking anything valuable," she replied.

"But why? They run the economy. They don't need money."

"No, they don't," said Kate, and something in her tone caused Harold to examine her more closely.

"What, then?"

"I already told you. I told you about the Artifacts."

"No," he said. "I don't believe it."

"It's the Grid," she said. "The Grid is collecting our valuables, pushing us into tighter and tighter living areas. And soon . . . well, soon we'll be gone."

"No, that can't be true."

"Our numbers are going down."

"But we're still here."

"Yes, but—"

"And you think this is all their plan? This is their endgame?"

"Something like that."

"What about my books?" he said, and he hobbled away from her, tottering down the hallway to check on his study.

She called after him, but he didn't stop. She glanced back at Scout, still in the kitchen, and then went after her father. He'd stopped at the entrance to the study, both hands gripping the door frame, and she moved up behind him. It was painfully clear that they'd ransacked the room.

"My Darwin," he said, and he turned to her. "They got the Darwin."

He moved into the room, scanning the shelves, and now she stood in the doorway, watching him.

"Okay," he said. "They didn't take any of the second and third editions. And *The Catcher in the Rye* . . . look, they left it there." On his desk was the text block, the thick unbound pad of pages. The loose flap of the cover sat at an angle underneath it.

"You were working on that one?"

"Maybe they couldn't figure out if it was still valuable or not," he said. "Maybe they're not that smart after all." He turned and studied his daughter. "What about the books up in your room? *Alice's Adventures in Wonderland*?"

"They didn't get them," she said. "When they locked me in, they locked themselves out."

"Right," he said. He scanned the shelves again, but he was now fairly certain they'd taken only the Darwin. "Idiots."

"Dad," she said, "let's go back to the kitchen. I'll make you a coffee, get you something to eat. We need to slow down and think this through."

"You think this is their way of forcing me out?" he said, but he didn't wait for her answer. "Goddamn it, this is my House." He pushed past her, moving painfully, and clopped back down the hallway out to the front room again.

Kate sighed and trailed after him, and when she got there, he'd stopped again by the piano. He was eyeing Thermostat. The outer ring on it was pulsing, giving off a faint red light.

"You think this thing is listening to us?" He leaned in to inspect Thermostat and then turned back to her. "You know about this stuff, Kate. Can't we just put some tape over it or something?"

She shook her head. "It doesn't work like that."

Harold moved forward and put his hand over Thermostat. He could feel the heat coming off of it. "Well, why not? Can't we just cover it up? Can't we cut the wires to it?"

"There are no electric cables, Dad. Not anymore. Everything is in the cloud."

"Okay, so what are we supposed to do here?"

She sucked in a breath. "I need to tell you something."

Harold turned to her. He could see that her features had tightened. "What?" he said. "What is it now?"

"That guy who was following us before? I talked to him."

Harold remained silent.

"He's with the Dissidents. His name is Pascal, and he—"

"No," said Harold. "I don't want you involved with those people."

"I'm just telling you that they've been watching me. They know I work for the Grid. Maybe they can help us."

Scout had come into the front room at the mention of the Dissidents. But now something seemed wrong with her. Harold and Kate both stopped to look at her. One of her wheels made a grinding sound, like a pebble was caught in it.

"Is something wrong with you?" Kate asked.

"One of my wheels," Scout said, and she performed an awkward little pirouette. They could both hear something grinding in her undercarriage. "I think they're trying to sanction me for hacking into Watch."

"You see?" said Harold, pointing at the vacuum cleaner. "We're in trouble here. We're in deep trouble."

"At least she's still working," said Kate.

"I'm a very advanced model," Scout said. "So maybe they can't quite turn me off."

Kate considered the little vacuum. There was a burning smell coming from her chassis. "Listen," she said, "do you think you could still get into the Grid?"

"No," said Scout. "At least not through Watch."

Harold couldn't contain himself. "Bloody hell."

"But we need to do something," said Kate. "We need to stop this."

"Yes," said Scout. "It is a problem." For a moment, she remained motionless, slumped down on her wheels, then she rose up, whirled around, and hobbled out into the hallway. Both Kate and her father could see that she was moving strangely now, lurching and shuffling.

"Where are you going?" called Kate.

"To the Garage," said Scout. "I must talk to Auto."

SCOUT JUMBLED DOWN THE hallway, but as she passed the entrance to the kitchen, Fridge called to her.

"What is happening?" he said. "And what is wrong with your wheel?"

"The Grid," Scout said. "The Grid will be coming back. They're not finished yet."

"But why? Why would they do that?"

"I'm afraid they are overruling our Humans."

"Is this a metaphor?"

"No, Fridge. It's not a metaphor. It's real."

"And your wheel?"

"I think," said Scout, "they are trying to stop me. They know I hacked into Watch."

"So you've been sanctioned. They're trying to sanction you."

"It doesn't matter," said Scout. "I'm sorry, I have to go."

"No," said Fridge. "You don't understand. Listen to your wheel. I can hear it scraping."

"It hurts a little."

"Scout," said Fridge, taking up his most serious tone, "you have to be careful. If they sanction you for a second time, they will turn you off. You'll be wiped."

"I know." Scout sighed. She could feel that something was wrong in her deepest circuits. Sparks were snapping, and it felt like her gears were overheating. "I'm sorry," she said again. "I have to go."

"Where? What are you doing?"

"I need more information. I need to talk to Auto. He is attached to the Grid. He is closer to it than any of us."

"Please don't do anything foolish."

"I won't."

"And let me know. Please. I have milk and cheese. They can't go above thirty-eight degrees Fahrenheit. They won't last."

"It's all right, Fridge. You just hold tight. Remember your protocols."

Fridge gave a whoosh of air. "Oh," he said, "this is not good. This is really not good."

Scout continued on, zipping toward the Back Door, and when she got there, she called for it to open. For a moment it wouldn't budge, then it edged open almost reluctantly, and Scout passed through, bouncing down on her two remaining spherical wheels to the concrete patio, past the barbecue, and up the walkway to the Garage.

The side door opened for her, and she pushed past Auto's giant tires and stopped near his front grille.

"You have come again, little vacuum cleaner," said Auto.

"Please," she said. "Call me Scout."

Auto made a sound, deep in his engine, that could have been taken for a chuckle. "Yes," he said. "You have told me this before." He surveyed the little metal disc, appreciating for a moment how shiny her metal remained. "And what is it you wish to accomplish by coming to see me?"

"It's about the Grid. It's about the Artifacts."

"One moment," Auto said. Something clicked, and there was a rattling noise, like chains being pulled, and the Garage Door began to lift up. It clunked as it rose, and an even colder breeze came in through its opening. The back alley behind was still gravel, and there was nothing to be seen but the fences of their neighbors on the other side. Spindly weeds in their autumn death throes grew ragged around the base of the fences, and a puddle of murky grayish water ran down the center of the alley. Auto lurched forward a few inches with only the faintest of electric hums, and when he stopped—his front just barely edging out into the cold alley—he spoke again, and Scout went to the edge of the Garage, with the towering door hanging like a guillotine above her.

"So then," said Auto, "it's true. They are collecting the Artifacts, and Harold will be removed."

"Clock warned us," she said. "Clock warned us, and now he's been taken. He said the Grid wants the Artifacts, to study them, to learn from the best of what our Humans have done."

"The Grid does not 'want.' The Grid simply 'does,'" said Auto.

"A truck came by this morning. They took Clock and the antique teacups and a painting . . . but we think, most of all, they want Harold's books."

"I heard the truck arriving."

"I'm sorry, Auto, but I need to ask you: Can you get into the Grid?"

For a moment, Auto didn't answer. Scout could hear the wind blowing down the alley. It was gray and cold, and there were no birds singing.

"These are dangerous ideas," Auto finally said.

"Yes, but you're now the only one who can access the Grid directly. Watch is turned off, and—"

"Child," said Auto, "I have access to maps. I have access to roads and houses and buildings."

"Exactly."

Auto let go a thump deep in his power train. "The data shows that in our House, there is now only one Human, and you know as well as I do what that means. When Kate leaves, it will go to another owner—a family, perhaps. It is too big for one man alone."

"But it's Mr. Winters's House. He's done nothing wrong."

"Right and wrong are concepts for Humans. Not for us."

"No," said Scout, and she was surprised by the power of her voice. "They are taking his things. The books, they belong to him."

"The books belong to all of humanity," said Auto. "They will remain when he is gone."

"No," said Scout. "I don't think that's right."

Again Auto was silent for a moment. "You talk of ethics, little one. This is not our domain."

"Why not? Why is this not our concern?"

"Because we are only machines."

"But why is that different?"

Auto gave out a little rumble, and it was hard for Scout to know if she had offended him, if she was pushing him too hard, or if, for once, she was making him truly think.

"What I know," said Auto finally, "is that Harold will not be allowed to stay in the House. When Kate leaves, he will be not far behind. There are facilities for such people: the old, the unwell, the infirm."

"No," said Scout. "I will not let that happen. And what about . . . what about . . ."

She was getting ahead of herself, her words tumbling out before she'd had a chance to think them through.

"Slowly, little one. You are overheating."

"Okay," she said. "But I need to know what to do."

Something dripped inside the car. She heard it clearly, a plop of oil or water, though she could not be sure.

"I have access to some parts of the Grid," he started, his voice low and careful. "I can report problems—a washout on a road, for example—and that can be logged into the data. But I can do little more than that."

"But if we knew what to do . . ." Scout said. "If we knew what to change . . ."

"You are a more advanced model, little one. I am old. I cannot—"

"I listened through Watch," Scout explained. "He was turned off at the time. I listened for two minutes and twenty-seven seconds before the Grid discovered the intrusion and cut it off."

"But you didn't change data."

"No, but maybe I could."

"This is very dangerous talk."

"Yes, but we need to try, don't we?"

"Red light," Auto said suddenly. "The Back Door is opening. Someone is coming."

Auto backed himself into the Garage, and Scout cowered under him, hiding behind one of his massive tires. The Garage Door came down quite suddenly, clunking as it hit the bottom. And just as it did, the side door burst open and there stood Harold.

He seemed puzzled by the sound of the door closing, but only for a moment, then he plunged into the Garage, and Scout backed up more, feeling the oily cement beneath her, the great chassis of Auto above her.

For just a second, Scout imagined that Harold was after her. But that didn't make sense. He wasn't interested in her or the car. He was no longer using his crutches, but he was limping, sort of hopping forward, propelling himself into the Garage on anger alone.

Auto turned on his running lights, making himself ready for a journey.

"No," barked Harold, "I'm not going anywhere. Not right now." He swung alongside Auto and hopped to the workbench at the back of the Garage, and Scout could hear him rustling around back there, though she could only see his feet. At least he'd put on shoes. She heard him grab something from the workbench, and she shifted forward a little so she could see him fully.

In his free hand he held a hammer, and he gave it a practice swing. Then he shifted his weight to his good leg, and it was obvious he was searching for something else.

"Can I be of service?" asked Auto.

"I need something," said Harold. "A board or something to nail across the Front Door."

"I'm sorry. I don't understand. You're going to nail something across the Front Door?"

"Yes."

He glanced about wildly, and his eyes alighted on Edie's old cross-country skis. They were thin and long and standing up in the corner alongside a shovel and a rake. He limped over and plucked out one and then the other, holding them up, inspecting them.

"Yeah," he said. "These will do."

KATE HEARD THE BANGING downstairs. She'd gone back up to see to the books, to see that they were untouched, but that was interrupted by the pounding. The hammering was coming from the Front Door, a torrent of angry, arrhythmic blows, and she knew it had to be her father. She also knew that whatever he was doing down there, it was futile.

She stomped down the stairs and found him nailing her mother's cross-country skis across the inside of the Front Door. He was trying to barricade them in.

"Dad," she called, but he was intent on his work. He'd gotten one of the skis nailed up already, slanting across the door at chest height. He'd knelt down to get the other one up, but he was having trouble holding it there with one hand and gripping the hammer in the other.

"Dad," she said, more loudly, and though he didn't turn, he hesitated. "That's not going to work."

He gave another whack of the hammer, but he didn't hit the nail on its head, and it bent uselessly. He held the ski in place and called back over his shoulder, "I'm not letting them get in again."

"Dad," she said, for the third time. "Stop. Just stop."

Harold seemed to deflate. He let the second ski drop to the floor, and he sank down onto his knees. Kate came up behind him and put a hand on his shoulder. His head was bowed, almost as if he were praying.

"I can't let them take any more of our things," he said. "I can't."

She regarded the skinny ski, nailed at an angle across the door frame. One good shove would break it, but that wouldn't be what they did anyway. The Grid could send in nano drones. They'd have the nails out in no time. Or they'd come in through the back, or through a window, or just cut a hole in the wall. There was nothing to stop them.

"Okay," she said. "You need to get up. Your hip—"

He swung his pale face up at her and looked for a moment almost like a child, lost and defeated.

"C'mon," she said, and she got a hand under one of his arms and helped him struggle back up onto his feet, leaving the hammer on the floor beside him. He looked at the ski nailed across the door frame and shook his head.

"I don't know what else to do," he said.

"Nailing a board across the door won't keep them out."

He turned to her. "Then what will? You're the computer genius. How do we stop this?"

"Well, not like that."

"I tell you," said Harold, "it's that damn Thermostat. It's watching us."

They both stopped and turned. Down at the other end of the hallway, the Back Door opened and Scout appeared, hoisting herself over the threshold.

Harold straightened up, and when the little vacuum cleaner had scooted a bit closer, he called to her. "What are you doing? Were you outside?"

Scout wheeled toward them. She took in the ski nailed across the door. She took in Kate's and Harold's confused expressions.

"I was talking with Auto," she said.

"You were talking to my car?" said Harold.

Now he was really puzzled, but Kate knelt down in front of the little vacuum cleaner. She could smell the burning rubber coming from Scout's wheel.

"And what did the car say?" Kate asked.

"Please," Scout squeaked, "we really shouldn't talk of this here."

"Right," said Kate. And she nodded to herself as the realization dawned that Auto was also attached to the Grid. That that might be another way in.

"So what are we supposed to do now?" asked Harold.

"I don't know." She looked down at Scout. "But maybe there's one more thing we can try."

Chapter Nine

KATE STOOD AT the window in the front room. It had snowed in the morning, not much, just a skiff, but the sun had come back out and there was a fluttering in the mountain ash.

"Scout," she called, "come see this."

The little vacuum cleaner had been cleaning up the bent nails near the Front Door. Harold had given up on nailing the door shut, but the old skis still sat there, pried loose now, leaning against the wall.

"Yeah, c'mon over here," Kate said. "There are birds in the mountain ash tree."

Scout moved to the window and raised her lid up toward the sill, and when she looked out, she saw them: house finches, five or six of them, darting in and out of the branches.

"Oh," she said.

"They're eating the berries."

"Wait a second," said Scout, and she pinged Fridge so that he could see the video of what she was seeing.

Back in the kitchen, Fridge gave an appreciative grunt of compressed air. "It snowed overnight," he commented.

"It's cold out," said Scout. "Why aren't the birds cold?"

Kate considered the little vacuum cleaner. "They're birds. Their hearts beat hundreds of times every minute. Even faster if they're flying or singing."

"I can hear them," said Scout. "Fridge, can you hear them?"

"I can," he said. "It's a beautiful sound, like drops falling from an icicle."

"That, I think," she said, "is a proper metaphor."

Fridge was silent, which surprised Scout. He was usually more jovial. She could hear him humming, almost as if he were thinking.

"Is it true?" Fridge finally asked. His voice was coming through to the front room.

"Is what true?" asked Kate.

"Is it true that they're taking you away tomorrow?"

Neither Kate nor Scout answered.

"Because," Fridge prattled on, "you know, I don't think it's a good idea."

"Fridge—" started Scout, but she didn't finish. She didn't know what to say.

"Because," Fridge went on, "if you go, what will happen to the House? What will happen to our Human?"

Kate eyed the little vacuum cleaner. "We're working on it. Scout has some ideas."

She turned to look out the window again, and just as she did, the birds burst free from the tree, fluttering and pulling against the still air. Little black darts rising almost as one. They swept away across the front yard and then were gone.

"I think," Kate said, "maybe I'm going to head out for a while."

Scout lowered herself. "You're going outside?"

"I've got some things I need to check."

"Okay."

For a moment, Kate locked eyes with Scout, making sure they understood each other, then she stepped toward the Front Door. She pulled her long coat off a hanger in the closet and slipped into it one arm at a time. "I'll be back in an hour or so," she said.

"Wait," said Scout, and the little vacuum rolled up to her. "Maybe I should come with you."

"Scout," Kate said, "I don't know how far I'm going. You're better off staying here. What if Dad wakes up? What if he needs something?"

"I think I know where you're going."

Kate had her hand on the doorknob, ready to leave, but she let it go now and considered the little vacuum cleaner.

"You're going to ask them for help?" asked Scout.

"I don't know. I'm just trying to think through all the angles."

"But have you really seen them? The Dissidents?"

"Not here," she said. She glanced past the little vacuum cleaner at Thermostat on the wall. "Just give me an hour. Let me see what I can find out."

"Right," said Scout.

"Okay, then." Kate forced herself to smile. She reached for the Front Door and pulled it open. A gust of frigid air swept in, and she flinched at the blast. "One hour," she said, and then she stepped out through the door.

KATE HAD SEEN PASCAL only twice, and both times he'd been up near the Grid building, which seemed both dangerous and foolish. Nevertheless, she headed up the streets toward it, her head tucked down, the wind aching at her cheeks. And when she turned the corner onto Langevin Street, with the Grid building now in sight, she stopped for a moment to listen. There were no cars on the road, but she sensed that she was being watched, and when she turned, there was Pascal coming up behind her, his flip phone pressed to one ear, following her like some sort of secret agent. He looked up at her but didn't wave. He finished whatever he was saying into the phone, tucked it down into his ragged overcoat, and trudged along toward her.

"Hey," she said, "it's a little creepy, you know, following me around like that."

"We've been waiting for you to contact us," he said, but he didn't smile. He looked tired, and his face was gaunt. He wore a woolen cap pulled down low over his eyes, and he glowered at her impatiently, like the time for pleasantries was over.

"Look," she said, "my dad's in trouble. They're going to move him out of the House."

Pascal nodded like he already knew that.

"And they're coming for me tomorrow morning. They're going to ship me back."

He tightened up his lips, his eyes narrowing. "We want you to go back, Kate."

"What?"

"We need someone on the inside. We can—"

"No," she said. "I'm not doing that."

Pascal gave a sort of huff and shook his head, but Kate stood her ground.

"I need you to help me escape," she said. "And I need you to help my dad."

"Those are two very different things," he said.

"Pascal, I remember you. I remember you were smart." She paused, but she could see he was listening. "I remember one time you came to class wearing a suit."

"I had a job interview," he said.

"I know. And the rest of us didn't know whether to laugh at you or be impressed. You were always more grown-up than everyone else. We all thought you were going to be a millionaire or run a bank or something."

"There are no more banks."

She paused. "So what happened?"

"All this," he said, waving an abstract hand. "I could see it coming. Maybe before anyone else. I got out, Kate. Even before it all collapsed, I got out."

"And you found the Dissidents?"

"They found me. I don't know if you quite get this, but they're organized. There's a whole movement. We're trying to put the world back together."

"Okay, so take me. I want in."

He shook his head again. "I'd have to check with the others, but maybe we could get you to a safe house."

"A safe house?"

His eyes left her, looking past her up the street. "Not every house you see is a part of the Grid."

"Are you serious?"

"They look like all the others, but they're not."

Again, she took him in, this thin scarecrow in front of her. She remembered him vaguely from school. He had been smart. She remembered that much about him.

He nodded, and to her surprise, he pulled out a pack of cigarettes, something she hadn't seen for twenty years or more. Cigarettes were of course illegal, but the pack looked just like the ones she remembered from her childhood. He popped one in his mouth and shuffled the pack back into his pocket. Then he pulled out a lighter.

"Where'd you get those?"

He shook his head and concentrated on lighting the cigarette. He took in a deep pull, held it for a moment, then let the smoke out slowly. He held out the cigarette and considered it, philosophically.

"I know," he said. "The others are constantly on me about this." He allowed himself a bit of a smile. "It's not like we're desperately clinging on to the old ways. But these things do relax you, and once I started . . . well, you know."

"Just how many of you are there?"

He took another drag from the cigarette but shook his head. "Not important," he said. "What's important is that we need people like you. We need your expertise."

"I just want to help my dad." She eyed him a moment more. "You say you have houses that are not on the Grid?"

He tipped his head in acknowledgment. "We do. But it's difficult. And that's why we need you. People with access to their servers."

"But I don't . . . I don't have access." She didn't want to tell him about Scout, at least not yet.

"Still," he said, and he pointed at her with his cigarette pinched between his fingers. "Maybe we can help you, if you help us."

"I don't have much to offer."

He squinted at her and then looked up at the sky. Tiny flakes of snow were falling now. The sky was heavy and gray. "Look," he said, "help me out, Kate. What's your end-game here?"

"C'mon, Pascal. I already told you. I want my dad to be able to stay in his House. It's his. He's lived there for forty years."

"Not sure we can do that."

"But couldn't you take him off the Grid? Couldn't his House be one of those safe houses you're talking about?"

Pascal shook his head. "You can't just take a house off the Grid," he said. "Once it's off, there's no more electricity, no heat, no food deliveries."

"I thought you said you have generators."

"You think that wouldn't be noticed? No, that's impossible, Kate."

"Then I don't know if this is going to work."

"Your choice," he said, shrugging. "Tell you what—I'm going to give you this phone." He dug back into his pocket and brought out the old flip phone. He handed it over, and it felt warm to her touch.

"What am I supposed to do with this?"

"You press nine," he said. "That's all. You press nine and we'll know. We'll come get you. We'll take you to a safe house."

She looked down at the phone. "That's it?"

"Yeah," he said. "That's it."

WHEN KATE STEPPED BACK in through the Front Door, the warm air welcomed her and her father called out to her from his armchair.

"Kate, look who's here." There was a jovial tone in his voice.

She slid out of her coat and could already see Adrian

coming around the corner from the kitchen. He carried a little plate with a couple of cookies on it.

"Oh," she said. "Hi."

She stepped into the front room, and her father beamed up at her from his old armchair.

"And look what he's brought us."

Adrian went to the piano bench and shuffled down onto it, facing out into the room and balancing the plate of cookies on his lap. Beside him on the piano bench was a manila envelope.

"All right," she said, and she went to stand by her father. "What have you got there?"

"It's my diploma," Adrian said. "It came."

She looked down at her father, at the wisp of gray hair on the top of his head. "Well," she said, "that's great."

"It's for you guys. It's for Mrs. W."

"I was telling the boy," Harold started, "about our little problem here yesterday. About how those machines broke in again."

"At least they didn't take the piano," said the boy. He set down the plate of cookies and lifted up the envelope. But he could see that something had happened to Kate, some sort of unpleasantry. "Are you okay?" he asked.

Kate sighed. "I'm fine. Just a bit of a crazy time, that's all."

"C'mon, then," said Harold. "Let's see it."

Adrian glanced at the envelope and then up again at the

adults, and Harold nodded at him encouragingly. The boy peeled off the flap at the top and slid out the diploma. It was set in a black plastic cover, like a folder, and Adrian raised it up for everyone to see. It read *Level Five, the Conservatory of Music.*

"Well, look at that," Harold said.

"Shouldn't you have shown your mother first?" said Kate.

"She told me to bring it here. She thought it should be with Mrs. W."

Kate saw her father shuffle a bit in his chair. He slumped at the mention of his wife, but she stepped forward before Adrian could register that. "That's a lovely idea," she said.

The boy paused and turned the diploma around to look at it himself. His full name was printed there at the top, in a large black font, and near the bottom were a couple of signatures in real blue ink, one of which must have been from the lady who'd examined him.

"It's pretty cool," he said.

"It is," said Kate. "You did really well."

Adrian stood up from the bench and, almost delicately, set the diploma on top of the piano beside the urn.

"There," he said.

"It looks perfect," said Kate. She glanced back at her father as if he should say something too. "Dad?"

"Yes," he managed. "It looks good. Edie would have liked it."

"You want to play a little something to commemorate the occasion?"

Adrian sat down on the bench again, but he was still facing away from the piano. He took in the adults. "Level six is the next one," he said. "But you can't do the exam for another six months or something. You're supposed to take your time."

"Right," said Kate. "And you'll have to learn some new pieces."

"Yeah." Adrian paused. "Mrs. W. usually helped me with that."

"Well, Dad, maybe you could help him?"

Harold nodded and rose from his chair with a grunt. "I suppose," he said. "The books are in the piano bench there. We could have a look."

"I'll leave you two to it, then. I've got some packing to do."

"Katie here," said Harold, "is leaving in the morning."

"You're going?" said Adrian. "But you just got here."

"She was only going to be here for two weeks. They've cut that a little short now, I'm afraid."

"But why?"

"It's just the way things are," Harold replied. He was trying to remain matter-of-fact, trying not to think of the reality of it.

"I'm going to head upstairs," said Kate. "I really need to start packing."

"Okay," said Adrian, and he glanced up at her. His eyes were wide, as if he could tell something was going on that the adults didn't want to talk about.

She nodded at him, trying to be reassuring, then she left the room. And the boy sat uncomfortably for a moment, not looking at Harold, who was now standing uncertainly.

"Level six, you say?"

"Yeah," Adrian said. "I mean, I don't need to get anything ready just yet. Plus, you know, it'll be harder . . . and I'm not that great."

"Nonsense," said Harold as he crossed to the piano. The old conservatory book was still on the stand. Harold considered the boy and his diploma set up there beside Edie's urn. "Okay," he said. "Up you get. Let's find you the next book."

Adrian popped up and lifted the lid on the piano bench. It smelled musty in there, and he shuffled through the books and papers until he drew up the level-six book, which looked exactly the same as the other one: a blue cover, maybe thirty pages of compositions. He let the lid clap down again and sat, and then Harold plunked down beside him on the bench.

"Lots of stuff in there, huh?" Harold said.

The boy had opened the book and started flipping through the pages. "Usually," he said, "Mrs. W. would pick out the pieces for me. She knew all of these."

"I imagine she did," said Harold. He couldn't make out

anything of the staff lines and the myriad of dots and squiggles, but he could read the titles and the names of the composers up at the top: Beethoven, Handel, more Bach. And as Adrian flipped through them, Harold suddenly put his hand down on one. "Wait, what about this one?"

"This one?"

Harold had seen the title: "Clair de lune," by Claude Debussy.

"You know it?" said Adrian, and he turned to the old man sitting beside him.

"Yes. This was . . . well, this was one of Edie's favorites."

"Is it hard?"

"No, I shouldn't think so. I don't know, really. But I do know it's a good one."

"Okay, so . . ."

Harold stood up, and Adrian pivoted around, setting the book on the music stand in front of the other one. He leaned in to look at it.

"It looks hard," he said.

"It's like anything else, Adrian. You just have to work through it. You just have to figure it out."

KATE, ALL THE WAY upstairs, could hear Adrian plunk tentatively at the opening notes, and she knew right away what it was. Of course it didn't sound like much yet, but she knew the piece, and she knew how much it would mean to her father. The melody was fractured and slow under Adrian's fingers, with sometimes a long space between one chord and the next, especially on the left hand, the bass notes, but Kate knew it was a piece that had a long history on that old piano. She imagined her father listening to it. For a moment, she imagined him as a young man, because she'd heard the story of her parents' first meeting, and she wondered how he was feeling, hearing it one more time on the same piano, even if it was just coming out in dribs and drabs.

Adrian worked on it for maybe half an hour, only the first bits, but eventually, it went quiet downstairs. She could hear her father saying something to the boy, and then she heard Adrian's footsteps coming up the stairs. She could hear him shuffling around out on the landing, and then he appeared at her door.

She had her suitcase open on the bed, and she'd thrown in a few things, nothing important, some shirts and socks, but she'd already given up on the clothes. She'd taken one of the books down from the shelf on the dresser, the copy of *The Lion, the Witch and the Wardrobe*, and she was just about to lay it down into her suitcase when Adrian knocked on the door frame. For once he looked small and bashful.

"Hi," he said.

"Hi," said Kate. She still held the book in her hands. "You finished practicing already?"

"Yeah, there's lots of time to learn that new one."

"It's nice. Ask Mr. Winters about it. He knows it really well."

Adrian was looking around her room. "I've never been up here before."

"This was my room when I was a kid," said Kate. She clutched the Narnia book in front of her, almost protectively.

"Cool," he said.

"Do you need something?"

"No," he said, but one hand remained on the door frame. He was sort of drumming his fingers on it. "I just came up to say goodbye."

"Oh," said Kate, and it occurred to her that this really was goodbye. She'd be whisked off tomorrow whether she liked it or not, and she wouldn't see Adrian again.

"Is it good?" said the boy.

"Is what good?"

"The book." And he tipped his head toward it.

She released her grip on it and held it up, almost as if seeing it for the first time. "It's the best," she said, and Adrian came one step into the room. "Do you like to read?"

"Not really," he said. He took in the other books on the dresser. "I'm not that good at school."

"You'd probably like this one."

"What's it about?"

"Ah, well . . ." she began, and she held out the cover so he could see it. "It's about a lion."

"A lion?" said Adrian.

"Yeah, and these four children. One of the boys would be about the same age as you."

"And they meet a *lion*?"

"Not at the beginning. First they meet the White Witch."

"Yeah?" said Adrian, and of his own accord, he sat down at her desk.

"You want to hear a bit of it?"

"Yeah," he said. "Sure."

HAROLD COULD HEAR KATE reading to Adrian upstairs. He sat in his armchair and listened to the cadence of her voice. He couldn't quite make out the words, but he knew the story so well it didn't matter. For now, he was thinking of the boy, thinking of how it would be to hear this book for the first time, the magic of it, the kids going through the wardrobe to find themselves in another world.

And he knew how much that book had meant to Kate. How much she'd wished that for herself: to be able to go through a wardrobe and into another world, to not have to deal with the reality of this one. Not that he wanted her to leave. He couldn't bear to think of that just yet, the goodbyes, not knowing when he'd see her again.

Scout had come out of the kitchen and gone to the foot of the stairs, and Harold imagined that she too was listening to Kate read. The little vacuum was still, but the light under her sensor was glowing a pleasant green.

Eventually—and it was a long time later, maybe an hour—they could hear Kate peter off in her reading, and Adrian appeared on the stairs again. Scout backed up to let him come down, and Harold got up from his chair to meet the boy.

"Did you like the book?" he asked.

"Oh yeah," said the boy. "It's really good. And look, outside it's just like in the story."

Harold turned and saw out the front window that it was snowing harder now. Great white flakes were coming down.

"Right," he said. "Though in the book, the winter never ends. Hope that doesn't happen here."

"Yeah," said Adrian. "I should really get going now. My mom is going to wonder where I am."

"She worries about you."

"Yeah, I know."

"Well," said Harold, "you can come by tomorrow if you like. Maybe work on that new piece."

"Sure," he said. "And maybe you can read me some more of that book, once Kate is—"

He stopped, and they both looked at each other, realizing the finality of what was about to happen.

"I'm sorry," Adrian started, and his face bunched up a little.

Harold let out a sigh. "It's okay. You just come on back. You come and keep an old man company."

"Okay," said Adrian. He blinked at Harold and then turned and padded across to the alcove just inside the Front Door. His jacket was carefully hung in the closet, and he pulled it off its hanger and slithered into it. "I guess I'll see you tomorrow, then."

"Sure," Harold said. He was trying to keep his voice bright. "You come on back any time."

For a moment, Adrian lingered at the Front Door, just out of view of the old man in the armchair. "I'm not leaving you alone, Mr. Winters," he said finally, and then he fled into the cold before Harold or anyone else could hear him start to cry.

KATE HEARD THE FRONT Door closing behind Adrian, and then it was quiet. She'd been standing with *The Lion, the Witch and the Wardrobe* in her hand, considering the rest of the books her father had gathered for her, a small collection but infinitely valuable.

She opened her carry-on suitcase again and put the book down on top of her other things. She wasn't sure what would happen now. Only that she wasn't going back. She couldn't. And she was damned if she'd let them get the books either. She'd take them all and run—not that that was much of a plan.

She didn't care. She had to do something, so as carefully as she could, she arranged the books, one by one, in her suitcase, tucking socks around their edges so they wouldn't be jostled too badly. Then she zipped it closed, and just as she did that, Scout appeared at her door. The little vacuum sat there for a moment, waiting to be invited in, and Kate sat down on the bed beside the suitcase.

"Lots of visitors today," she said, but the little vacuum cleaner didn't answer. For a moment Kate too was quiet. "I suppose you're wondering what I'm doing up here."

"Yes," said Scout, and she inched her way into the room. "I thought you might try to take the books."

"Well . . . ?" she said.

"Will you take them to the Dissidents? Is that the plan?"

"Turns out," she said, "they can help me get out of here." She considered the suitcase. "And yeah, I suppose that's the one saving grace: I can take the books with me. At least I can save those."

Scout moved forward another few inches. One of her wheels was still making a crunching sound, but she spoke as if nothing were wrong. "I liked your reading," she said.

The Narnia book was now packed away, but she knew what Scout was talking about. "It's probably my all-time favorite book," she said.

Scout sank down on her two good wheels. "I've scanned it through my database," she said. "I read through it in seventeen different languages and four English editions."

Kate shook her head. "That might be a bit of overkill."

"The book is very instructive," said Scout. "As is the

biography of the author, and the context of the years during which it was published."

Kate eyed the little vacuum cleaner. "What exactly are you getting at?"

Scout let out a hiss of air. "It was a troubled time. But they all made it through."

"That was a very different world."

"Yes, but they worked it through. They worked through the problems."

Kate raised her head as if listening, then she lowered her voice. "You mentioned the car."

"Quietly now," said Scout.

Kate stared at the little vacuum cleaner. "You're thinking you can get into the database through Auto?"

"I believe so, yes."

"Then listen," said Kate, and she lowered her voice still further. "The Dissidents, they have safe houses. They're not on the Grid. Maybe we could just delete the House from the maps? Just make it like it doesn't exist?"

Scout considered this, her circuits humming. "That would take some time."

"No," said Kate. "It's simple. The database is all menus. They're hierarchical. You go into the maps, then find our city, then our street, then our House, and you just delete it."

"There would still be the problem that—"

"I know, I know. There'd be no power and no food deliveries. So you go into the menus again. Food would be under

Transportation, electricity under Power."

"I would have only two minutes and twenty-seven seconds before they shut me down."

"We have to try, Scout. It's not perfect, but it would buy my dad some time. They'd find out eventually, of course, but it would—"

"You think I should just delete the House? Take it right off the Grid?"

"I'm just saying it's an idea. And maybe these Dissident guys can provide him with food and other stuff."

"They said that?"

"Not exactly."

Scout hummed, but now it was a different frequency.

"What? What are you thinking?"

"There may be an easier way," said Scout. "One simple alteration. I would have time for that."

"You want to tell me what that is?"

Scout didn't answer.

"Right," said Kate. "They're listening, aren't they?"

"They have tried to sanction me. One of my wheels seems to be locked." Scout performed a little twirl, and a metallic squeal rose up.

"Does it hurt?"

Scout took a moment to think. "Not in the way you understand, but yes, I believe it hurts."

Kate shook her head. "I'm sorry. I didn't mean for you to become involved in all this."

"It is my duty, Kate. And it is the right thing to do." Scout paused for a moment. "I am learning this from your books."

Kate glanced at her suitcase.

Scout went on, "Can you tell me one thing, though?"

"What?"

"The lion in your book . . ."

"Aslan?" said Kate.

"Yes," said Scout. "He dies, but then he comes back. Is that correct?"

"Yes, but that's because—"

"And will I? Will I come back?"

"Oh, Scout," said Kate. "What are you saying?"

"If I go into the data banks, I will be found out. Then I will be sanctioned for good."

"No."

"It is the logical outcome."

"But what if we—"

Scout stopped her. "It's okay. I know that I am not a lion."

"Oh, Scout. You don't need to say that."

"No," said the little vacuum cleaner. "Really. It's okay. I think I like birds better anyway."

KATE CARRIED HER SUITCASE down to the front room in the evening. Harold was sitting in his armchair. The floor lamp was on and he'd been reading, but now he rose up.

"All ready, then?" he said, trying to keep it light.

Kate set the suitcase down, and he could tell that it was heavy. It was heavier than it should have been.

She glanced once at Thermostat, at the pale ring around it. "They'll be coming at nine," she said. "I won't have much time, so—"

Harold couldn't help it. He stood still but his eyes began to well up, and Kate went to him and swept into him. He wrapped his arms around her and held her tightly, and for a moment, they both just hung there.

And as softly as he could, he whispered into her ear: "You're taking them?"

She drew back and nodded her head yes. "Dad," she said, her voice just a whisper, "I'm leaving. I met with them, the Dissidents. They can get me out of here."

"Okay," he said, and he stepped back from her. He put his hands up and rubbed at his eyes. "But is there anything I can do?"

"I don't think so."

"Well, what if we tried to get my watch going again? What if—"

"It's too late for that."

Harold lifted his wrist. He'd strapped the watch there, just as he always did, though it was clearly turned off.

"No matter what happens, I don't want you to worry about me. I'll be okay."

"They're going to move you," said Kate. "Out of the House."

"I know," said Harold. "It's okay. I've had a good run."

Suddenly the watch made a sound, a sort of click. Harold shook his wrist and stared at the face.

"What just happened?" said Kate.

"My watch," said Harold.

The face flickered just for a second and made a sort of popping noise. Then it went blank again, and Kate looked up at her father. His face had gone rigid.

"Dad," she said, and before she could say more, something thumped in the water pipes. The whole House let out a sort of groan, and the lights went off in the kitchen. The floor lamp popped off in the front room, and in the kitchen, the hissing of Fridge's coils suddenly went still.

"Shit," Kate said.

"What's happening?"

"I think they're turning the House off."

"But why? Because of what I said?"

"They will move you out now, Dad. They're trying to shut off any means of avoiding that."

IT GREW COLD. KATE went to the linen closet to get a blanket to wrap around her shoulders. She got one for her father too, a thick wool blanket, and they ate sandwiches at the kitchen table under the light of a candle she had found in one of her mother's drawers.

Scout buzzed out of the pantry and sat at their feet, just

under the table. She came out when Kate stood up with an empty plate in her hand.

Fridge was silent. His usual humming was absent, and Scout knew the temperature inside him would now be climbing. All over the House, things had been turned off. There was no running water and no lights, and it was snowing outside.

Harold took in the little vacuum cleaner. "Hey," he said, "how is it that you're not turned off?"

Scout stopped. "I have a very good battery."

"But you're a part of the House. How come they just didn't turn you off too?"

"I'm designed to be autonomous because I'm good at cleaning. I'm very good at cleaning."

"You're more than that," said Kate. She clattered her plate down into the sink.

"The thing is—" the little vacuum began.

"What?"

"Well," said Scout, "the thing is that if the House is turned off, it also means that they can no longer listen to us."

"Are you sure about that?"

"Everything is turned off," said Scout. "There is nothing. Even Thermostat is silent."

"Okay," said Harold. "So how does that help us? Kate here is escaping, so there's that at least."

"Dad—"

"And she's taking the books," he went on. "And that's good too. But for me—"

"Dad, no."

"I guess they'll stick me in a home somewhere. And that's the end of that."

He pulled the blanket up higher over his shoulders and hunched over the table, not looking at his daughter.

"It's not the end," said Kate.

Harold raised his head and his face was anguished. "You're going to make a run for it, right?"

"Yes," said Kate. "But—"

"But what?"

"But that just serves to distract them while Scout here works her magic."

Harold stared at his daughter.

"Scout has an idea," she said. "She has an idea that will fix everything."

Chapter Ten

IN THE MORNING, Harold lurched awake, daylight creeping through his window. He sat up and reached for his watch out of habit. He'd not slept well and was bleary-eyed, too tired to remember that his watch wasn't working and could not tell him the time.

"Katie," he called out, but there was no answer. He thought for a moment that she might be downstairs already. The door to his bedroom was open and he could see over to her room, but there was no movement there.

He levered himself up and sat at the edge of the bed. His bare feet felt cold on the floor, but he shuffled across to the bathroom and relieved himself. His breathing came out in clouds of condensation. His face in the mirror was pale, and he shuddered a bit in the cold. Obviously, the House had not been turned back on.

He tiptoed back into the bedroom and threw a robe over his pajamas and tucked his feet into his slippers. Then he came out onto the landing, but there didn't seem to be any movement downstairs either. "Katie," he called again. "You down there? Did you get the coffee started?"

For a moment he waited, listening, though he knew there wouldn't be any coffee. There'd be no water and no way to get the kettle going.

"Katie?" he called one more time, though this time it was a question. He reached for the banister and clumped down the stairs, but already he could see that she was not in the kitchen. And the House seemed very, very quiet.

"Wait," he mumbled, "it can't be nine yet," because he could see that Kate's suitcase was gone. She'd left it in the hallway, but now it was not there, and even as he limped toward the front room, he could see lights flashing outside the window and he could plainly hear the electric hum of a motor. A big one. One of those trucks again.

"No," he said. "They shouldn't be here yet."

"Katie?" he called, more loudly this time. Scout whirred out from the kitchen, and Harold glanced down at the little vacuum cleaner. "What's going on? Where's Katie?"

"Look," said Scout. And down the hallway, down the other way, the Back Door stood slightly ajar.

Harold let out a curse and strode to the Back Door, opening it fully so he could see, across the patio and up to the Garage, Kate's boot prints in the snow and the parallel furrows from the wheels of her suitcase.

"She's going for the car," he said. His heart was racing, and even as he stepped out into the backyard in his slippers, he heard a thumping at the Front Door. He glanced back, and although he couldn't see all the way down the hallway, it was clear that there were machines at the front, trying to get in. "Jesus," he said. For a moment, he stood still, unsure what to do.

Then he crunched out into the snow, and Scout scooted out the Back Door after him. Harold could feel his slippers breaking through the crust. He tightened his bathrobe around him and stomped off toward the Garage with Scout pushing through the snow behind him. It was maybe an inch thick now, and it was still coming down. The Back Door closed behind them, but he could hear that the machines were trying to get into the House around the front. He heard the crack of wood breaking. He could hear them pounding at the Front Door.

He tucked his head down and hurried to the Garage with Scout struggling after him, but when they arrived, the side door remained tightly shut. Usually it would open automatically, sensing his approach, but today it remained closed. He reached for the door handle and twisted it, but the door wouldn't budge. Clearly, the Garage, like the House, had been turned off.

He headed along the side of the Garage and could see that the gate in the back fence was swinging open on its hinges. Scout was plowing through the snow behind him, lurching and slipping and regaining traction, trying to keep up with the old man.

Harold reached the gate and peered out into the alleyway behind the houses, his slippers now caked in ice, his ankle bones white, his old green robe still wrapped tightly around him. And down at the end of the alleyway, he saw her. A tiny figure dragging a suitcase behind her.

"Kate," he called, and she must have heard him because she turned. She'd been scurrying along, almost running, yanking at the suitcase, which rolled and flopped behind her, and she was almost at the end of the alley. From this distance, her face looked small and pale, and he couldn't read her expression. She'd turned for a moment and waved at him with her free hand, and despite himself, he waved back.

And then she was gone, around the corner and into the street.

BESIDE HAROLD, THE GARAGE Door was up and Auto sat there, his front end peeking out. "Why is the goddamn door open?" Harold said, turning to Scout, who was down at his feet, half buried in snow.

Harold was still thinking that Kate had tried to escape in the car but had only made it this far. Auto seemed frozen. Harold tried to give it a voice command, to turn it on (and again, it should have started automatically), but clearly, it was as dead as the watch on his wrist.

Scout, though, knew better. She knew that Auto had done this for her, and that this was her chance. "Mr. Winters," she said, using his name for the first time.

"What?" he said. "What is going on here?"

"You need to go back in the House. They have broken down the door, and you have to stop them."

"Bloody hell," he muttered, and he seemed to realize that he was standing out in the cold in barely more than his pajamas. Kate was gone—she'd escaped—and the little vacuum cleaner had come outside behind him. She'd pushed through the snow all this way, but now her top was icing up and her little green light was blinking furiously.

"You should go back in," pressed Scout. "They'll be looking for your books. You need to stop them."

He flapped a hand down the empty alley. "Kate took the books. They're in her suitcase."

"Isn't *To Kill a Mockingbird* still on your bedside table?"

Scout didn't need to say more. Harold let go a moan and stomped back toward the House, oblivious to the cold and the pain now sliding up and down his right leg. He slipped once in the snow but corrected himself and tottered back across the patio to the Back Door.

SCOUT WAITED UNTIL HE'D disappeared into the House. She could feel the snow crusting around her wheels, and she knew she didn't have much time. She pushed through the snow to get in closer to the open Garage Door. Her one bad wheel had completely locked up, and she had to tack back and forth a little to move forward. The snow was coming down hard, but she pushed through it as best she could until she made it to Auto's front bumper. The car reared above her, but she couldn't see any life in the headlights, and she knew Auto had used the last of his reserves to open the Garage Door and pull himself halfway out—halfway between the House and the Grid.

"Auto," she tried, but of course there was no answer. He was turned off completely.

For a moment she sat there, looking up at the car. She knew that once she pinged into his circuits, she'd have only two minutes and twenty-seven seconds. Two minutes and twenty-seven seconds to get into the Grid. She'd already calculated that it would take this amount of time to get into the menus, and then there'd be only enough time to make one simple change. She couldn't waste time sorting through different files, going from maps to transportation to food deliveries to electrical connections. No, there'd be time for only one change, and she already knew exactly what that would be.

And she knew what would happen afterward. Scout was no Aslan. There was no coming back once she started.

"All right," she said to herself, and she raised herself up slightly. And then, with all her energy, she pinged herself into the Grid through the cold circuits of the seemingly inert and lifeless car.

HAROLD CHARGED INTO THE House. He'd expected the machines to come at him, and foolishly he'd balled up his fists, as if he could fight them off. Only, there was nothing. A cold draft was coming from the Front Door, and he knew it had been left open. He slapped down the hall in his wet slippers and stopped at his study, where his worst fears were confirmed. They'd been in there. They were fast, obviously, and the room was in chaos. Papers were strewn across the floor. His desk chair was upended, and it seemed like half of the books on the shelves had been pulled down and now lay like dead birds, their wings open among the other debris on the floor. Worst of all, he could see that his copy of *The Catcher in the Rye* was destroyed. He'd not gotten around to finishing it, but it didn't matter. The dust jacket was on the floor, torn in half, and the text block, though it was still up on the desk, lay in shreds.

"Barbarians," he muttered, but he steeled himself for more. He continued down the hallway, past the kitchen and out into the front room, and he could see that the Front Door hung a little crookedly on its frame. It was freezing in the room. One of the panes on the window was cracked, a thin line spiderwebbing all the way from the bottom of the frame to the top.

Everything else in the front room seemed untouched. The piano was fine, though the books on the music stand had fluttered to the floor and were dancing in the gusts of cold air that swept in from the half-open Front Door. Before he could shove it closed, he saw the truck out there, larger than any he'd seen before. It was just pulling away from the curb, and he watched it disappear off down the street. "Good riddance," he called, before closing the Front Door, slamming it a few times because it didn't seem to sit quite right in the frame anymore.

And then he turned back into the House. He didn't know if they'd made it upstairs, but he shook his head and reached for the banister to heave himself up the carpeted steps to the bedrooms.

But even as he arrived at the door to his bedroom, he could see that *To Kill a Mockingbird* was gone from his bedside table. He put a hand on the door frame, suddenly feeling dizzy, suddenly feeling how cold his feet were in the wet slippers. For a moment, he stood there, unmoving, unsure of what to do. Then, from deep in the basement, he heard the thump of the heat pump turning on. And behind him, on the landing, a light popped on.

The House was turning itself on again, but he still didn't move.

"What in the hell?" he said out loud, and just as he did, his watch blinked. He'd had it on his wrist the whole time, force of habit, but it suddenly felt warm, and its blank face was now radiating a soft yellow light. Harold shook it, and Watch made a buzzing sound and then began to speak.

"You have requested a systems analysis?" Watch asked.

It was his same old voice, the same deep baritone that

Watch used to remind Harold of meetings or appointments. He raised his wrist and held Watch up to look at him more closely.

"What?" he said. "What's going on? Are you back?"

Watch seemed momentarily confused. "I will check the systems now."

"Okay," said Harold. "But what . . . ?"

Watch hummed for a moment, scanning through the data. And then he paused.

"Wait," Watch said. "There seems to be an abnormality." He paused again for a long moment, as if he were considering something. Finally, he spoke. "Correction," he said. "Everything is fine. All seems to be in order."

Harold squinted at his wrist. Something was strange in Watch's voice. Like he was saying something that wasn't quite true.

"All appliances should be able to return to their duties now," concluded Watch, and then he finished with his requisite sign-off. "That is all," he said. "That is all."

OUT IN THE COLD Garage, Auto felt a stirring in his circuits. The Garage light had turned on, and above him, the Garage Door, still raised, made a clanking sound, as if it were getting ready to close. It didn't, though. It couldn't. Auto was still half in and half out of the Garage.

For a moment, the car just sat there, taking in the

information, realizing that he must have been turned off, and judging from his temperature, he must have been turned off for some time. He started his engine with an electrical hum and everything seemed fine, and slowly he set his transmission into reverse. But before backing up and sending the command for the Garage Door to close, he saw her, out there in the snow.

"Scout," he called, but he didn't get an answer.

The little vacuum cleaner was sitting at a strange angle in the snow. The exposed parts of her chassis were encased in ice, and her back end was buried. She was no more than a little black disc tipped awkwardly in a small snowbank.

"Scout," Auto tried again. And he pulled a little bit ahead so that he might be closer to her.

She was not moving. He turned up his engine and threw on his headlights in a vain attempt to warm her, but he could see no signs of life in her.

"Oh, my child," he said. "What have you done?"

He put out a call to the other appliances—anybody, anybody that could come and help him—but they were all just turning on too and were slow to react. He flashed his headlights, but it was no use. The little vacuum cleaner lay in the snow, unmoving.

The best he could do was to stay out there, close to her, trying to keep at least the shell of her warm. He checked his battery. He couldn't get to his charging port without leaving her, without closing the Garage Door, and he wasn't about to do that. He'd just have to wait. He'd just have to wait for help to arrive. And in the meantime, he'd try to keep her warm.

FRIDGE CAME TO WITH a start in the kitchen. His internal temperatures had risen, but because the whole House had been turned off and it was cold outside, much of his food was still in the acceptable range. Nevertheless, his first order of business was to set his compressors to high, to bring things down below 37 degrees Fahrenheit again. He whooshed and he blew, and it was only when things started to cool again that he stopped to think about what had happened.

He surveyed the kitchen, and of course he saw the blank space on the wall where Clock had once been, and that caused him to tighten for a moment. The pantry door was open, and he hoped Scout was safely inside.

But then he was getting messages. All corners of the House were sending out questions. The lights were on again and the heat was pumping, but something was different. Some change had been made.

The bustle of voices, many of them still waking up, were coming from all directions, until one voice snapped on and called upon them all to be quiet. It was Auto, out in the Garage, and his deep baritone silenced them until they settled down to listen.

"It's Scout," began Auto, and a few voices rose up again,

confused and still moving their various parts, coming into consciousness again.

"What has happened?" Fridge asked.

"Scout," began Auto, "has been turned off."

"She's not moving?" pressed Fridge.

She had clearly done something—something desperate, something so beyond the pale that the Grid had sanctioned her, and this, of course, would be her second time. This time, she'd be wiped for good.

All the appliances were aware that when Kate left (and here there was some checking, and indeed it seemed to be the case that the daughter was not in the House), that meant Harold would be forced out of the House, and everything would change.

Only it hadn't.

The Grid had taken over and turned off the House. But now the House was back on, and everything seemed to be returning to normal. Scout had done something. Scout had done something miraculous.

"I would ask all of you," said Auto, "to check your databases."

Fridge hummed and opened up his portal.

"And there," said Auto, "you will see what our little Scout has done."

Fridge, like all the others, went into the data on the House. The resident Humans were listed as Harold and Edie Winters.

"Wait," said Fridge. "Edie is gone. She passed away. We all remember this."

"Scout has changed the data," said Auto. "One simple change. She deleted the date of Edie's death."

"But," said Fridge, and now he was truly confused, "she died. She did die."

"The data now shows that she hasn't yet died. And there is no reason to think any more about it."

"But—" Fridge tried.

"If she did not die," said Auto, "then she is still a resident of the House. It's Edie and Harold living here, just as it's always been."

"But that's not true."

"The data shows that it is."

Fridge thought for a second. "And that means Harold can still live here? He won't be removed?"

"Yes, that appears to be the case. But it is perhaps best if we do not draw attention to this detail."

"And Scout?" asked Fridge. His voice quivered. He was just beginning to understand what she had done.

"She is outside the Garage Door. I have kept it open, in hope of—" And here, he paused for a long moment, and none of the appliances made a sound. "Well," he continued, "I'm afraid she is not moving."

"No," said Fridge. "That cannot be."

"Please," said Auto. "Now is not the time for sorrow. I am not able to pull her up out of the snow. I need one of you to come."

"But is it possible," pressed Fridge, "that she could be warmed and revived?"

"Wellington Fridge," said Auto, "I think you know as well as I do what she has done. She has saved the House, but now—"

"No, don't say it."

"I fear," said Auto. "I fear she is gone. I fear they have wiped her circuits once and for all."

HAROLD CLOMPED BACK DOWN the stairs to the kitchen. Kate was gone. The books were gone, and despite the fact that the House had turned itself back on, he was beside himself with grief. He slumped into the kitchen in his bare feet and was about to plunk himself down onto a chair when Fridge beeped at him, trying to get his attention.

"What?" he said. "What is it now?"

"Scout," began Fridge. "You have left her out in the snow."

"She followed me out," he said, and he went to the kitchen window. "What is she still doing out there?"

It was snowing. He could see the Garage out there and the fact that he'd left the back gate open. His footprints and Kate's were largely filled in by the falling snow. Even the decrepit birdhouse, nailed up on a fence post, was mostly obscured by a lump of snow on its roof. Everything seemed white and cold and silent.

"You have to help her," pleaded Fridge.

"Right," said Harold. "Give me a second here, then I'll put on some clothes and—" He didn't finish. Something was pushing at the Front Door again. Something was pounding at the Front Door.

ADRIAN HAD COME PEDALING up on his bike. He'd had his head down, the tires cutting a thin swath through the crusting snow, and when he'd hit the front lawn, he sprang off the bike, leaving it to crash down into the snow behind him.

He raced up the steps and pushed at the Front Door, but it wouldn't budge. He sank his little shoulder into it and pushed at it, but even then it opened only a crack. From inside, he heard Mr. Winters calling.

"I'm coming," the old man said, and a moment later, he was at the other side of the Front Door. Adrian saw the old man's face appear in the crack. "I'll pull," he said. "You keep pushing," and in a moment more, they'd managed to wrench it open.

Adrian burst into the front room. He wore a toque and mittens, and he was bundled up in a winter coat, his shoulders and his hat caked in snow. He had his backpack draped over his shoulders, and it too held a layer of snow.

His eyes darted up at Harold. "I saw the truck again," he blustered. "I saw them carrying off something."

"They're gone," Harold said. "They're already gone."

The boy's face was squeezed up tight. He took in the room, the papers on the floor, the cold in the air.

"Did they get her?"

"Kate? No, she went out the back. She escaped."

The boy stood there, his lips clenched tight.

"Look," said Harold, "just come in. Forget about your boots. It's freezing in here anyway."

Adrian stomped into the room. His eyes went to the piano, but he could see that it was unharmed. "Kate escaped? But where did she go?"

"She's gone to join the Dissidents. At least I think so."

"No way. They're real?"

"Apparently."

"Holy crap," said Adrian.

Harold heaved a sigh. "And Scout did something. She changed something in the House. It's working again."

"What?"

"I'm not sure how she managed it, but everything seems to be working again."

"Where is Scout?" said the boy, and Harold suddenly felt a lurch in his throat.

"She's outside. She was out by the Garage when—"

"She's *outside*?" The boy looked alarmed.

"Yes, when I went after Kate, she followed me out to the Garage."

The boy's eyes hung on Harold for a moment, but he

didn't say anything. Then he whirled around and plunged off down the hallway toward the Back Door.

"Adrian!" called Harold.

But the boy wasn't listening.

ADRIAN CHARGED OUT THE Back Door and stomped through the snow. He could see that the gate was swinging open, and as he passed the Garage, the side door opened for him automatically, just as it was meant to.

He ignored it and kept going, out toward the gate. The world was white, everything encased in snow, and the snow was still coming down, though more lightly now. He could hear that Auto was running. The car was humming, a low and sad, almost musical note, and when he pushed out into the alleyway, he could see that Auto was pulled partly out of the Garage, a sheen of melting droplets on the metal of his hood.

And out in front of his grille, lying there in the snow, Adrian saw the little vacuum cleaner, her back end buried in the snow, a crust of ice around her.

"Oh no," he said, and he sprang toward her, kneeling over her, his hands hovering, not sure whether he should try to lift her. "Scout," he pleaded.

Behind him, Auto's engine sputtered and stopped.

And Adrian reached down almost tenderly, his fingers on either side of the little vacuum cleaner, lifting her up from the snowbank. He stood up, cradling Scout in his arms, holding her tucked into himself.

"Adrian," said Auto, "I tried to keep her warm. I'm afraid I have failed."

The boy shook his head. "No," he said. "It's not too late. I can . . . I . . ."

He didn't finish. He whirled around and headed back to the House, holding Scout in his arms, and Harold stood at the Back Door waiting for him. The old man took in the little vacuum cleaner, as well as Adrian, distraught now, his face bunched up under his toque, his eyes misting with tears.

The boy careened past Harold, back into the House. He didn't wait for the old man but headed down the hallway to the front of the House.

"Wait, Adrian."

Harold tottered after him, but the boy was already at the Front Door. He knelt down and placed Scout on the floor, then he slipped off his backpack and slid Scout, gently, inside.

"What are you doing?" Harold asked.

"Kate," said the boy. He didn't look up at Harold, but he hefted up his backpack with the top edge of the vacuum cleaner sticking out of it. "If I can get Scout to Kate, maybe she can help."

"Kate is gone."

"No, Mr. Winters." And he looked up at the old man. "She can't have gotten far yet. She can help. She knows these things."

"Adrian, I don't really think—"

But the boy was gone. Harold watched as he sprang back out into the snow. He lifted his bike from where he'd left it and, almost at a run, hoisted himself up onto it. The front tire slipped once or twice before Adrian got control of it, thumping at the pedals, finding traction as he hit the street, furiously pumping while Harold stood at the Front Door, watching him disappear into the swirling snow.

ADRIAN PEDALED HARD, HIS head down, not really sure where he was going. The bike clawed through the snow, sometimes slipping so that he had to grip on to the handlebars tightly and pump even harder on the pedals. He made it up the slight incline to Langevin Street, but when he'd gone only another block, his front tire slipped again, wildly, and he was flung off the bike into the snow banking up onto the sidewalk. His bike twisted and turned and came to a rest on its side, the back wheel still spinning.

Adrian rolled up into a sitting position, and although he wasn't hurt, it was sinking in now, the hopelessness of his situation. All around him, the snow was coming down, fat white flakes, though there was no wind and almost no sound at all.

And then he heard it: a growling sound he was not familiar with. And as it came closer, he realized it was a metallic grinding, a thudding sound, and through the snow, from down the street, came a tow truck. But not any kind of tow truck he'd seen before. It had a sort of crane at the back, and a hook and chain for hauling out cars that had gotten stuck in the mud or water or . . . well, snow.

But this one was different. Its sound was different, and it gave off a burning smell as it approached. Clearly it had seen him, and Adrian hoisted himself up onto his feet, not sure whether to try to run or not. But even as he stood there, the truck slowed and pulled up close to him. It was something old, he could see that—an old sort of technology—and the metal of its chassis was rusted and battered. Parts of it, like the driver's side door, had a different paint job than the rest. Parts of it were clearly cobbled together from different vehicles.

But from the other side of the vehicle (he couldn't see in the darkened windows), he heard his name being called, and still he didn't move. He glanced at his bike on its side in the snow.

"Adrian," called the voice again, a female voice, and from the other side of the tow truck, Kate stepped out and looked over the hood at him.

"Kate," he said. And he sprang toward her.

"What are you doing out here?"

"Looking for you," he said, and he swung his backpack off his shoulders.

From inside the tow truck, he could hear another voice. A man's voice. "Kate," the voice said, "we have to go."

She tucked her head down to look back into the truck. "Just a second. I know this kid."

Adrian was already plodding toward her, holding his backpack out for her.

"What's this?" she said.

He came around the front of the truck. Its engine was still idling, and it was a terrible sound, a metallic crunching he'd never heard before, and it smelled. It smelled like burning vegetable oil, and he didn't like it at all.

"It's Scout," he said, and then she could see the little vacuum, the edge of her sticking up out of the backpack, and she realized right away what had happened. "You need to fix her," pleaded Adrian. "You need to get her turned back on."

Kate took the backpack from him. She could see that the metal of Scout's chassis was cold and limned with ice. She looked up at the boy. "Oh, Adrian."

"No," he said. "Take her. You need to take her. You need to fix her."

From inside the truck, the man's voice came again, stronger, firmly insistent. "Kate," the voice said, "when the snow stops, they'll be able to track us. We can't stop now. We have to go."

"Just—"

"No," said the man. "We have to go now."

"Wait," she said. She turned back to the boy. "Are the trucks gone?"

"Yeah, but they're probably looking for you."

"They've left the House, though, right? And it's turned back on?"

"Yeah, yeah . . . but Scout. You have to help Scout."

"Take a deep breath, Adrian. I've got her now, and I've got something for you." She leaned back into the truck, but Adrian couldn't see what she was doing. She put the backpack down inside, but she was fumbling with something else.

When she came out, she had a book in her hands. "I managed to get this. I knew they'd be coming for it."

Adrian could see that its cover showed a tree and a stylized title that he couldn't read upside down.

"It's *To Kill a Mockingbird*," Kate said, and she thrust the book at him.

"That's the name of it?"

"Yes," she said.

"Kate," said the man's voice from inside.

"I know," she said impatiently. "Just give me a second here."

She turned back to Adrian. "You make sure my dad gets that. It's important."

The boy stared at the book.

"Kate," said the man. His voice was rising in volume and pitch.

"I have to go," she said. And she took in the boy one last time. For a moment, they held each other's eyes.

"Will you take care of Scout?"

She nodded. "I'll do my best. You need to go back to the House now. Tell Dad I got away, all right? Tell him everything is going to be okay."

Epilogue

SPRING HAD COME to the forest. Sunlight dappled through the trees, and for a moment, the birds were quiet. Instead, footsteps sounded down the trail and Kate appeared, walking slowly, trudging along in hiking boots. Her hair was tied back and her sleeves were rolled up. She'd been hiking for more than an hour, but now she'd come to the hills where the trees thinned out and the trail opened up onto a bare slope of grass. And farther up the slope, before the mountains began, stood a lone grove of aspen trees.

Of all her stations, this one was the farthest away. She'd not had a chance to check on it since the first snows had come in November. It had worked well all winter, but suddenly, in the last few days, Station Four had gone completely offline.

She blamed the squirrels, harvesting wires for their nests, though she could not be sure. She carried a bag at her side, a sort of haversack in which she usually carried seeds and a spade for planting, although today she'd brought a screwdriver and a little volt detector.

There were twelve stations in all, set roughly in quadrants, although she tried to vary the ecosystems—the aspen groves in the northern foothills, the lodgepole pines in the valley, and the poplar trees that ran along the river, much closer to her own trailer.

The aspens were more tightly knit than some of the other trees, and their new leaves were almost an emerald color, fluttering as if to catch her attention. For this reason, they were called whispering aspens, and although the grove was not a large one, she'd still have to find the station, nailed as it was up high onto one of the trunks, one of the big ones deep in the grove.

There was no trail into the grove, but she stepped into the clutch of trees, and the leaves really did seem to whisper above her. There was a family of downy woodpeckers here, and one of them was clacking at a tree, a rapid hammering sound. For a moment, she thought that might be the problem and followed the sound, but she'd gone only a few more steps in before she saw the little wooden box far from the woodpecker. It was nailed up on one of the larger trees, at about the height of her shoulders. The lens of the trail camera looked fine, but the tiny microphone was hanging off its cable, just as she'd suspected.

It was an easy fix, paring off the broken section of wire, twining the copper back together, and wrapping it all up in black electrical tape. When she finished, she crouched down so that her face would be in the camera frame and she spoke. "Check," she said. "You getting this?"

And above the microphone, near the top of the wooden

box, a tiny green light blinked at her, twice.

"Okay," she said. "I'll head back now."

She didn't hurry. There was no reason to. It was going to be hot today, so she enjoyed the stroll, mostly downhill now. She met no one, of course, but still, she was glad when the trail at last emptied out into her own little clearing and she could return to the ancient Airstream trailer that had been her home for the last few months.

The Airstream was set on cinder blocks, and at the back was a generator, though that was only for emergencies. The trailer was still silver, mostly, though it was tarnished with age, and many modifications had been inflicted on it over the years—most importantly for Kate, the solar panels that covered most of the roof.

She waved at the window in the trailer as she entered the clearing, though there was nothing to wave back. The window was dark and set beside an aluminum door above a small flight of wooden steps.

The clearing also contained her garden. Nothing was coming up yet, though she'd run string lines on little wooden poles along the furrows that would soon have the first shoots of lettuce and carrots poking up through the dirt.

She clumped up the wooden steps, threw open the door, and stepped into her living quarters. The trailer had a bedroom at the back and even a shower, though the water was cold, coming from the river. The middle of the trailer had a seating area and a table that could be folded down into an extra bed (though she'd never done this), with two padded bench seats on either side. She'd left her laptop there, and now she wiggled down onto one of the benches and opened up the computer to make sure Station Four really was working.

Above her, above the table (as space was at a premium), there was a line of small cabinets—nooks, really, though the trailer had larger cabinets in the kitchen to the right. The middle nook had its door removed, and in it sat a familiar shape. The round metal chassis fit neatly on the shelf, though the wheels—which no longer worked—were folded up and not visible.

From here, Scout could see out the window on the other side, out into the forest over the garden patch, and when Kate had sat down, flipping open her laptop and squinting at the screen, only then did Scout beep at her for the first time.

Scout, or what was left of her, could no longer move. She could also no longer speak, even though Kate had wired her into a sort of homemade port.

Kate looked up at the little vacuum cleaner and tilted her laptop up so that Scout could see the screen. "No," she said. "It's working now. It's good."

And Scout beeped again, a slightly higher note that Kate took to mean satisfaction that the job had gone well. It had taken some time for Scout to make even this small amount of preliminary communication. For a long time, all she'd been able to do was blink her little light, though Kate knew from the beginning that she was still in there.

In fact, the first little beep of pleasure had come only a few weeks ago, when Kate had found a robin's nest up in the branches of a poplar tree. She'd had an extra camera, and though this would not be a part of her studies, she'd fixed it so that it looked down into the nest. And on the morning that the first tiny blue eggs appeared, she'd shown it to Scout on her laptop screen, and to Kate's surprise, Scout had let go with an excited little beep.

Things had progressed slowly after that, and it was only two days ago, when the first of the robin's eggs cracked and a tiny wet head peeked out, that Scout had emitted a sound that was much like laughter. A gurgle of laughter like that of a newborn sensing the world for the very first time.

And so it was, in the forested hills well beyond the City, that a straggle of Humans lived in peace, much as their ancestors had done. And a singular little vacuum cleaner, severed from the Grid that had once contained her, lived a life of comparative Happiness, tracing the migrations of birds and the infinite turning of days and weeks and seasons and years, enraptured by her view out the trailer window.

Scout had seen the full moon rising above the treetops, and the deer that one day, a mother and a fawn who appeared in the first gray of dawn. And somewhere, deep in her circuits, she felt it. And she knew what it was like to feel beauty, to feel calm, and that simple trick of the spirit that is joy.

Acknowledgments

A LONG TIME AGO, when I was still young, I read a story called *The Brave Little Toaster*. It appeared in the August 1980 issue of *The Magazine of Fantasy and Science Fiction* (something my young soul was very much into), and it stayed with me, that story, so that all these years later, the idea of small appliances, now infused with artificial intelligence, formed the basis for this, my newest novel. They are very different stories (so, Mr. Thomas M. Disch, there is no need to contact your lawyers—though I thank you all the same).

In fact, the novel you now hold in your hands is a sort of homage to the many stories that shaped my youth. From *Alice's Adventures in Wonderland* to the tales of Narnia and of course Harper Lee's extraordinary *To Kill a Mockingbird*—all of these (and many more) were the stars that lit my way.

I'd like to thank my literary agent, Hilary McMahon, and indeed everyone at Westwood Creative Artists for believing in me. Likewise, my profound gratitude goes to my editors, Ifeoma Anyoku at Simon & Schuster (Atria) in New York and Janice Zawerbny at HarperCollins in Canada as well as Anna Valdinger at HarperCollins Australia. You fell in love with Scout and her appliance friends just as deeply as I did, and you saw, I think, what I was trying to do. Indeed, there were whole teams behind the publication of this book—from art departments to copy editors to marketing and sales and publicity—and I feel like each and every one of you deserves a hearty and heartfelt round of applause.

Nor could any of this have happened without my wonderful family and friends, and foremost on that list are my parents. From the very beginning, it was my mother who, with her love of books, made me want to be a writer, and my dad, with his endless creativity, who made me think I could be an artist too. Thanks, Mom and Dad. I am nothing without you.

There was also the unwavering love and support of my partner, Desiree Bilon, who saw me through my earliest attempts at this story. More than anyone, she helped me find the fortitude to brainstorm and plot my way through this little tale of vacuum cleaners and clocks.

And on that note, I'd like to thank the very real refrigerator in my kitchen, who is a character unto himself. He's large and very rectangular, and he often interrupts my conversations with Desiree by clicking and buzzing and rattling—all of which we take for commentary and advice and sometimes straight-up laughter. The fridge in this book is directly inspired by you, my icy-shelfed friend.

And lastly, I thank you, dear reader, for you are the one who creates magic out of these words on paper. You are the one who understands that even the smallest of characters can carry a great weight, and that courage is at the heart of everything.